CATCHING *FIRE*:

A TRANSLATION DIARY

First published by Charco Press 2022
Office 59, 44-46 Morningside Road,
Edinburgh EH10 4BF

A CIP catalogue record for this book is available from the British Library.

ISBN: 9781913867256
e-book: 9781913867263

www.charcopress.com

Copy-edited by Fionn Petch
Cover designed by Pablo Font
Typeset by Laura Jones
Proofread by Fiona Mackintosh

2   4   6   8   10   9   7   5   3

Daniel Hahn

CATCHING *FIRE*:
A TRANSLATION DIARY

CHARCO PRESS

For Diamela Eltit, and all the other writers who have entrusted their precious work to me. With thanks, and just occasional apologies.

Introduction

I am a literary translator.

OK, but what does that actually entail? Well, to put it most simply, my job is to read a book in language A, and write it again, in language B. I read with all the sensitivity, insight and analytical acumen I can bring to a text, and then I create a new thing, one that's identical to the original book, except for all the words. A new thing, to allow a book I've loved to meet new readers.

One might imagine translation to be an intimidating thing, a sort of miracle of baffling complexity. But let's not start there. Because on the most basic level, translation is those two things, each of them simple enough, after all: *translation is reading*, and *translation is writing*. In a sense, there's really no more to it than that. Translators read a text, then write another text. Read something in Diamela Eltit's Spanish, say, then write something in my English. Yes, doesn't that sound simple enough?

When translators work on a text, then, they are typically in negotiation with two languages, but they engage with each of them altogether differently. Language A is the one they consume. Language B, they produce. Inhale… and exhale. Translators have to be – at the very least – brilliant readers in one, brilliant writers in the other. Each of these tasks can be demanding, obviously. You do whatever it takes to work out what's happening in this line of Greek, Tamil, Welsh; to see what it is, the *something* that's happening beyond the mere words of Language A; and then marshal all your sophisticated Language B skills to write that something, in Vietnamese, Korean, Dutch. So translators are hybrids – a particularly strange kind of reader, with a particularly strange kind of writer. They read *through* a film of words to that thing that lies behind them – and they write that thing. They read *Die Prinzessin auf der Erbse* – and beyond that veil of words, they find… a princess, and a pea. And they tell that story.

Of course, some translation actually is straight-forward. Flat, cliché-ridden writing can be pretty easy. Characterless prose stuffed with set phrases can be easy. Lazy, unoriginal writing can be easy. Anyone can do that. (Which is why so many do, alas.) Translating a hackneyed phrase, easily slipping out one tired old Urdu idiom and comfortably slipping in a dull English equivalent to replace it, is, like any cliché, money for old rope. But the good stuff is different. Good writing isn't about easily interchangeable set phrases. That's not the bit that sets the translator, or the reader, alight. Good writing, the writing that's a joy to read or to translate, is new and unlikely, replacing cliché and formula with something altogether fresh, brightly lit and alive.

Any well-chosen word, when pressed into service, will do many things at once. It may be conveying semantic data, but it'll also be doing it in a certain way – a tone of voice, diction with particular characteristics, the placing of stresses, the number of syllables. A whole web of cultural associations will trail after it. Echoes of other words. Sounds that help a reader understand what might not be explicit. Which is not to say that every writer does all these things deliberately and consciously, but if the writing is good then they'll be there. And if the translation is good, they will all *still* be there after we've had our way with it – *all* those things will remain intact for a perceptive and curious new reader to discover. And unlike writing intended merely to convey data, artful literary writing is the kind where all those other things actually matter. So I want to keep them all in my translations. People think about translating as a process of de-coding, which it is; but it's also about re-*en*coding. Not just deciphering a meaning, but reconstructing a new expression for it. And that second part, the intricate re-encoding, is usually the hard part – and why I love it.[1]

Sometimes the constraints we're working to are particularly stringent. The whole novel has to be in iambic pentameter, or all of the words have to start with vowels, or it's full of palindromes,[2] or every eleventh word has to spell out the lyrics to "The Battle Hymn of the Republic". It might have pictures, so the new text needs to be in dynamic conversation with them, too. Or maybe it's just been written by Diamela Eltit. But even something that's not linguistically inventive or tricksy or showy or ludic will demand impossibilities from translation. We know this obviously about poetry – which I seldom translate, being basically a coward – but all prose that has artistry to it does just the same.

Even the very best translators will acknowledge this: essentially, theoretically, translation is impossible. It's one

---

[1] I mention this because I'm not sure the diary you are about to read conveys how much I love it. There's, um, quite a lot of complaining. But don't be fooled.

[2] I have in fact done this and don't recommend it.

of the paradoxes inherent in literary translation, I think. It's easier to do it, or at least to do it well, once you've understood that in theory it cannot be done.

Which is fine. I'm totally sanguine about this impossibility.

I've seen maybe twenty Hamlets; some have been uninspired or incoherent, and some great, and with the great ones it is possible to assess and appreciate each for what it is, rather than the ways it falls short of impossible perfection. In reality, every performance is partial: a reading, an interpretation, and then an expression. Translations are just like that. They can be good, or very good, or really breathtakingly good – but there will always be something that they aren't doing. Your performance of Hamlet might be ground-breaking, but there will always be something in the part that you weren't able to contain within it, however sophisticated and capacious your reading.

Each individual performer of a play script or musical score finds different things in that source, renders it in a unique way. Can a translation be perfect, include *everything* that's there? Of course it can't. No more can a performance of the Goldberg Variations be *perfect*, no more can a production of *King Lear*, no more can a poem. Does that mean we don't try? There's no perfect translation of a single word, let alone a complex 48,000-word novel. Perfection isn't even the metric we should be using to think about it. How tiresome to be still stuck with the idea that every translation should be measured against some notional perfect translation and always, inevitably found wanting. Instead of measuring it against its own aspirations or, well, against not existing at all.

If I asked you to complete the phrase BLANK *in Translation*, you would – just admit it – replace the BLANK with the word "Lost". Translation is so often measured in terms of loss. But I think my work allows things to be *Found* in translation. Freed in translation. Recreated in translation. Reimagined. Reborn. Rediscovered, restored, *revived* in translation.

Umberto Eco called translation, "the art of failure", after all, didn't he? And fail we must, with every syllable, insofar as the fact that we're changing it all means, you know, that we're *changing* it – but far better one great actor's interpretation of Hamlet than never to see it performed even a single astonishing, imperfect time.

Like an actor performing a part – a common metaphor for the work of a translator. Either that or we're ventriloquists. Or ghost-writers, or bridge-builders, tightrope-walkers or conductors or smugglers or shadows or musical arrangers or chameleons. Every translator has a favourite metaphor to help to convey the rigours and joys of this strange profession, a metaphor that usefully captures the interpretative element, the flexibility, the dependent relation to the source text, the impossibilities and opportunities. None of these metaphors is more than a partial match, but they can be useful nonetheless.

My own personal go-to metaphor? Translation is like copying a work of art in a different medium. We're art forgers attempting to reproduce an oil painting using only pencils, but so skilfully you won't be able to tell the difference. Imagine copying a watercolour, but using pastels; or a charcoal picture, using only pen and ink. You want it to look the same, but you can't just copy brushstroke by brushstroke; different media, like different languages, have different strengths and facilities. Different ways of creating an impression of light, or perspective, or density, or texture; languages are just the same. When writing a piece of English you have recourse to a different set of tools from those used by the Spanish-language artist – but you want the impression, *somehow*, to be unchanged. That "somehow" is wherein lies the skill and the apparent mystery, of course.

Because that's what makes it hard, isn't it? Making a cheese sandwich isn't difficult, but making something that will fool you into thinking you're eating a cheese sandwich using a set of ingredients that doesn't include bread, butter or cheese but nonetheless *precisely* replicates the taste, smell, texture, aftertaste... When I embark on translating, say, a Chilean novel, I know I'll have to recreate it as identically as I can, *except* – and here's the trouble – I'm not allowed to use Spanish to do it. And English is not the same! There's no word in one language that maps perfectly onto a word in another language, and every language has things it's good at and things it just can't handle. Replace French word x with English word y, you might find y a good, brilliant substitute; y might indeed be more interesting, doing more interesting things than x; but y is never x.

Now, a simple example. A basic word. You'll learn early on in your French classes that a *book* is a *livre*, which is obviously true, and also completely not true at all. *Book* is certainly the basic word that English people use to describe this physical object sitting beside me on the desk (bits of printed paper bound together along one edge); and as any dictionary will tell you, the default word a French person would use to tag that same object is *livre*. Or rather, *le livre*, because you're far more likely to present the noun with the article in French. Not to be confused with the adjective *libre*, meaning *free*. Free to do something, that is; free of charge, in French, would be *gratuit*. As opposed to, say, costing a pound, which is also, wonderfully, a *livre*. Oh, and if it <u>weighs</u> a pound, that's *livre*, too – but in that case, I think, the noun is now feminine? A good, multipurpose word, is *livre*! It does so many things. Only one of which is the same thing that *book* does – pointing at this object on my desk.

For an English speaker, our *book* overlaps in that one function (thing-on-desk), but then does all its own other things. It's the basis of idioms (brought to *book*, throw the *book* at him, in his good *books*, take a leaf out of her *book*…); it's a verb, meaning approximately the same as *to make a reservation*. It also sounds like "book", rather than "livre" – *book* rhymes with *crook* and *nook*. (There's a bookshop I like in Brighton called The Book Nook, so I feel that's important.) It has the same long vowel sound as *good*; and, at least in my particular English, it doesn't have the same vowel sound as *boo* or *moon* or *food*, though it looks like it ought to. If they asked me I could write a book, about the way you walk and whisper and look; which is all very well, but the charming sentiment only works if we're operating in English. French books don't rhyme with looks. French books rhyme with *ivre* (drunk); and French books are quite like lips, which are *lèvres*, or maybe hares, which are *lièvres*.

Every time we write a word, it does many things. Things to do with conveying data (=bound-paper-thing-on-desk!) but also conveying association, and sound. Even a word that doesn't do the multiple semantic duties that *book* does, will still be one-syllable long or three, with big or small sounds, hard or soft, it will or won't remind us of certain other words, it'll relate in a certain rhythmic way to whatever comes before and after it; it might be a word that tastes like *electricity*, or, quite differently, a word that tastes like *moon*. (And as I mentioned, in literary translation, many of these things beyond hard meaning, things like sound and colour and texture, are significant.)

So – *livre, lièvre, nook, electricity*. Those are the words; always translatable in part, always untranslatable in their entirety. Each substitution loses sounds and associations, and *gains new ones*. The last book I translated had about

85,000 Portuguese words in it and 92,000 English words in the translation; if so much is lost and gained with each one of those little transfers, not to mention every potential comma (though I admit I almost certainly will mention them later), how can it possibly be the same book?

Translation would be significantly easier if we only had nouns and those nouns only meant one discrete object-thing each. There's a thing – pages, binding, ink – on the desk; those people have a word for it, and so do we. But even then, we'd be assuming that the image that comes into your head when a reader in Manchester sees the word *tree* is the same as the image conjured in a Brazilian person by *árvore*. Or that the associations of the straight-forward noun we call God/bird/musician/moon/tribe were the same as the semantically equivalent nouns in other languages. Well, so much for that. So – in short – even down on a word-by-word level, there's no single word in one language that maps perfectly onto a word in another – not one. And every language has things it can do, and things it can't.

Think, for example, of those languages whose word order is flexible, which might perhaps allow a writer to move all the verbs to the end of their respective phrases, and hence save up surprises, an effect that's harder to achieve in English. An Anglophone translator like me can't just neatly say "I went into town today, where I a movie watched, and a pair of shoes bought, and a quick cup of coffee and a sandwich poisoned." So I would need to exercise a certain amount of ingenuity, putting in quite a lot of effort to muster up an effect that would have come very easily to the author of my source.

The former model and media star Katie Price – making a surprise appearance in this Introduction – is named as the author of a number of books. This kind of "authorship" is interesting to me. As *The Sun* newspaper reports it, "Katie is honest about the fact that she doesn't write the books herself – she says she comes up with the plots and the characters before leaving the typing to someone else." As a translator, I think "the typing" is quite important.

We translators have somebody else telling us what our sentence has to do – convey this piece of information about a character, say, but very succinctly, in a distinctive high-register voice with a slight note of scepticism, a sprig of parsley and some elegant phrasing that sets up the contrast with the abrupt shock sentence that follows – and we just have to figure out *how* to do it, using *our* language. We read book A, and then we write book... A. (Book A and book A having no words in common but being otherwise identical.)

It's an incredibly *writerly* challenge. And the *writing*, for me – that's the pleasure of it. It's a piece of new writing, and re-writing, at once. You might think of it as writing the book I believe the author would have written if they'd been writing a book in English. Or to put it another way, they are the ones who work out what the book is, it's all them – I'm just the guy who comes in at the end to do their typing.

(Incidentally, I warmed to Hunter S. Thompson considerably when I learned that he typed out *The Great Gatsby,* end to end, before he'd ever written a book of his own, just to see what it felt like.)

Early-career writers are constantly being told that the most important thing they have to do is to *find their voice*; but one of the things that makes us translators different from, say, most novelists and poets, is that our struggle, when we embark on this career, is not to find our voice, but to lose it. By losing it – an art that really *can* be quite hard to master, you know, Elizabeth… – we can venture out unencumbered on the hunt for somebody else's. But what *is* desirable is that the translated writer does indeed have his or her own distinctive voice-in-translation. (Just as an actor, being dubbed, is usually dubbed by the same voice-over performer, film after film; if you're an Italian cinema-goer you don't want the actor who looks like Russell Crowe suddenly to start speaking with the voice that over the years you've attached to Woody Allen.) Margaret Jull Costa's Saramago translations are recognisable; her Javier Marías translations, too. But you'd never confuse one for the other. Each of those writers has his own English voice now, in just the same way that each has his voice in Portuguese or Spanish. And just as I would hope to recognise a passage of Saramago in Portuguese at two hundred yards, I'd expect to recognise a passage of Saramago-via-Margaret-Jull-Costa in English. In these versions Saramago is, if only temporarily, an English writer, the literary DNA that's embedded in his/ her new and hybrid voice coherent and unique.

And it's never a neutral act, of course. It cannot happen without context, and it can't happen without interpretation or personality, however much we may *think* we're trying not to leave fingerprints. In her attempt to write the same thing a writer wrote, a translator will employ more or less of her own creativity and more or less of her own insightfulness and more or less of her own suppleness of language, ingeniously recreating all the things that Spanish does naturally but in another language that does all things differently. In short, writing someone else's book, but backwards and in high heels.

Give two translators the same non-English text, we'll come up with entirely different sets of English words, with versions in which every sentence is different. The individual variances themselves may be trivial, but great writing is composed of instances of brilliance that are cumulative even if they're individually tiny: the spring in a flat poetic line moved one syllable this way or that, a half-breath that can have disproportionate, breath-taking effect. Defining the difference between *talk* and *speak*, or between *little* and *small*, might not be easy to do. And nor might it be easy to explain just what the difference is between "And so that afternoon he left." and "And so, that afternoon, he left." And yet those two tiny commas are significant in their effect. Do I use *little* or *small*, *talk* or *speak*, do I add the commas or don't I? Each of these is among a thousand personal micro-choices that a translator will make.

In an early issue of *Asymptote*, the novelist David Mitchell wrote: "As a writer, I can be bad, but I can't be wrong. A translator can be good, but can never be right."

Quite so. Translation is the sum of its choices, choices that are more or less persuasive, more or less justifiable, but always subjective. Because translators are individual *interpretative* readers and individual *creative* writers, rather than just lexicographical datasets or collections of algorithms. So when we've done our reading, the real work is in the writing. Finding creative ways of reconstructing something that's every bit as witty/elegant/jagged/anachronistic/languid/wry/slushy/plodding/acrobatic as the source, and in precisely the same way.

But if, as I said, languages are all different – and therfore translation is impossible – how then can we get away with it at all? Well, it works because all effective translation is also sleight of hand. While someone reads a translation I've written, in that moment I don't particularly want them to be aware of my role in the process. I don't want them to think about the extra layer of mediation I represent in their dealing with the original author. On some level, I want them to think they are reading the original – that, I feel, should be the experience of any translation-reader. Ask them if they've read *Madame Bovary* by Flaubert and the answer should unthinkingly be "Yes!", even if they've really only read a version that was actually written by some modern-day American woman. (That "only" is dangerous, I know.) The ideal? For me, the ideal is a reader getting to the end of Diamela Eltit's *Never Did the Fire* and thinking *Wow, but – wait – hang on a second – but I don't speak Spanish – what happened there?*

If asked, sure, you know perfectly well that it's a translation, of course you do; just as, if you were to stop the performance, the audience could tell you that, no, that man up there isn't *really* the Prince of Denmark, he's just some guy pretending. But if he's doing it right, while you're within the story you inhabit the performance as though he were the real thing, unmediated. Yes, unmediated – that's the word. Readers should feel they're getting unmediated access to a work of art, even if they know – once you've brought the houselights back up – that they aren't. It obviously doesn't mean you cannot interrogate and appreciate the performer's part in your experience. But that sense of direct access to the writer's creation should still feel true at the time – the translation/performance feels not like its substitute but its revelation. But is the work's re-expression really the same thing as its source? No, nor could it ever be. Like I said: sleight of hand.

What it is, is a new piece of writing, seeking to create the same effects as the original but using entirely different tools. And the way this works (this strange *fidelity* we talk about so much) is another neat little paradox: to keep it just the same, we need to change all of it.

So I think of translation as an optimistic act. Rather than talking in terms of loss – what *hasn't* come through?

how's the translation inferior to its source? – it's refreshing to consider the opposite, as we translators must always do. What is it that survives? And in particular, how is it that something like "style", which we attach so closely to the specificities of linguistic activity, can survive being wrenched out of a language entirely and re-made in another? Diamela's prose has so much of its own literary *style*. Yes, an optimistic undertaking, if ever there was one.

It's worth mentioning that among the multiple ways in which it is a practice of *gains*, translation can be a potently activist endeavour – not merely responsive, quiet, deferential. Translation is about making certain voices louder; about pushing at borders till they stretch; about poking at the cheap and easy idea that a national culture is monolithic, an idea that all translators know – all readers know – is hollow. (Why any culture would *choose* to be hermetic and thin and bloodless rather than porous and capacious and teeming I can't begin to imagine – it eludes me, it truly does. And yet, here we are.) Translation acknowledges linguistic and cultural borders, but believes there are things more important. It celebrates language, but is built from those things that transcend language. Tolerance, mutual understanding, the transfer of progressive ideas, innovation – all the things that make cultures thrive can, sometimes, be *gained* in translation, carried in with the work.

And I think of translation as an aspirational craft, too. In the sense that what it intends is somehow pre-determined, so the process is one of reaching towards that thing, trying to come close to it, as close as different languages and individual skill and circumstance allow. I don't believe one can make a perfect translation, obviously; but I do know what – in the abstract – would characterise a perfect translation of a novel if one could – I know what such a thing would be. (Or perhaps, what it would *do*? If fidelity is a useful notion here at all, what I am seeking is fidelity to what I imagine to be the source text's *effect*.) This doesn't mean comparing every translation to its notional perfect and finding it inevitably lacking, it simply means – what? – being clear about the direction of travel? There's some impossible horizon towards which the process is headed, each draft inching nearer. The idea – abstract again – of *what translation is* will determine the criterion behind those countless choices. Which of these two options will take me closer, which will do what I think a translation ideally should do?

That's just me, though. There's plenty of discrepancy, even among translators, in our determinations of what translation is. My sense of reaching towards a patently impossible "perfect" thing already betrays my own feelings about the relationship a translation should have to its source. And certainly when I call my piece of work a translation, the claim I'm making for it is about just that relationship – my translations are translations because they aspire to be impossibly the same as another text. Broadly speaking, the more *the same* they can be, the better *qua* translations. The process of arriving at that new text is exploratory, iterative – you start with a text, and you painstakingly find your way back to it. And the end-product, with any luck, looks like art.

The million-dollar question, of course, is "How do you get there?"[3]

I've always loved "The making of…" as a genre. Behind-the-scenes access, rehearsal footage, actors' diaries. One of my favourite books about the theatre is Antony Sher's *Year of the King*, which is all told-from-the-ground experience, all trial-and-error, all in-the-moment

---

[3] Well, at current rates, actually *the 145-dollars-per-thousand-words question*, but whatever.

observation and process and craft. Mystification I find less interesting. But the nuts-and-bolts craft that lies beneath the surface of that thing that looks like art? In his Actors' Studio interview, Stephen Sondheim explained that as a young man, he still believed in The Muse, until he went to college "and [professor] Robert Barrow was talking about leading tones and diatonic scales… and I fell in love. He took all the mystery out of music and taught craft – and within a year I was majoring in music."

One of the reasons that aspiring to a pre-existing perfection is all fraud, of course, is that a translation has no life independent of its maker. (Even though I admit to finding the pretence useful.) I would have written this Introduction differently a month ago. Sondheim and Tony Sher died very recently, just a few days apart, which is surely why both are in my thoughts. And the Me of ten days hence would have evolved to draw on slightly different resources again. Translation is just the same. Certainly, reading back over this diary a few months on, in preparation for its book publication, I'm surprised to re-discover some of the choices I made earlier this year ("what – *really*?"), and variously amused, impressed and alarmed at the things I chose to care about. Like everyone, I have good days and bad days. Days when I'm more distracted or more focused, better attuned or worse, sounder in judgment or, um, less so.[4]

Peter Jackson released his massive Beatles documentary trilogy, *Get Back*, in the same week that Sondheim and Sher died, a co-incidence which means that it, too, happens to be part of my personal how-to-explain-the-world lexicon and at front of mind as I write this Intro-

---

[4] This time last year, you thought keeping a diary of your translation process was a good idea. Just saying. *(Ed.)*

duction on this exact day. At one point in the first part of the movie, there's footage that shows Paul McCartney just kind of conjuring the song "Get Back" out of the air, out of nothing. (A hat! Where there never was a hat!) It is a perfect display of genius, of inexplicable artistic *instinct*. It's an astonishing, dazzling moment and I love it – but it teaches me nothing about song-making, other than "Step 1: Be Paul McCartney." (Which I am not.) But so many other sequences in the same trilogy show us stage-by-stage developments, a lyric or a bit of instrumentation or a chord sequence evolving gradually in discussion.[5] This is no less marvellous to watch, but it also makes useful sense to those of us who cannot fall back on being song-writing geniuses.

Craft, unlike inspiration, is explicable, and hence learnable. Its moments can be slowed down, isolated into discrete choices. One choice after another, one word after another, watching all the moving parts doing their thing, even when you're working with a tool as maddeningly fiddly as language.

Hence, then, the possibility of this diary, which describes the process of translating a novel, covering three and a half months at the start of 2021. It was originally published online, on the Charco Press website, even as the translation was underway, so it was written to be read entry by entry, in real time.[6] It is best consumed, then, only in occasional short bursts.

I have tidied up the diary very lightly for this book publication, but I've resisted the temptation to do too

---

[5] "All of you hold a chord of A, then you creep up with the drumming … Then get to the G … Now try syncopating a bit … That's to rhyme with 'station', you know … The middle eight then into B-flat …" and so on.

[6] This fact might help to explain some otherwise weird things like me telling you in this book to "Have a great weekend!" and similar.

much. The odd infelicity, inconsistency or repetition is compensated for, I hope, by preserving the immediacy of the process. A translation does not develop smoothly, predictably, neatly – or at least, it doesn't for me – and what might seem an occasionally shambolic diary is a more honest representation, I think, than something that suggests premeditation, predictability and order. Progress is sometimes halting; but you can be reassured, the translation *will* get done in the end.[7] If you want to find specific subjects, there's a not altogether comprehensive index at the back.

The process shown in this book is not supposed to be instructional. It is merely a description of what I do, not a prescription for anyone else. My way of working won't suit everybody's temperament, or their circumstances; and indeed I'm sure there are plenty of very good reasons to do things quite differently. But I hope some readers – translators and non-translators – will find it an interesting process to watch all the same. Most importantly, of course, I hope you'll read the novel itself, and love it just as I came to love it while producing the translation; and these small insights into how the English-language version ended up taking the form it did might perhaps enhance that pleasure just a little.

The diary, and the translation process, began just under a year ago, on January 23, 2021.

---

[7] Spoiler! *(Ed.)*

23 January

Why a Diary?

This week I start translating *Jamás el fuego nunca*, a short, intense novel by the Chilean writer Diamela Eltit. It will be my main piece of translation work for the next two or three months, and my Charco Press friends and I have decided to invite you along for the ride.

Jamás el fuego nunca is currently a Spanish-language novel. By the time this diary ends, it will have become an English-language novel called *Never the Fire Ever*. The new novel won't have any of the same words as the old one, but I'm hoping it will be otherwise the same book. Whether we get there – and, if we do, *how* we get there – well, we shall see.

But why a diary?

(Apart from a natural translator's desire to make things more difficult for himself – and, you know, ego?)

I think translation is amazing. And it's sometimes a very difficult thing to do well. But it's not, I think, mysterious, or at least it shouldn't be. When we translators are working successfully, we're doing something that's incredibly intricate, and delicate, and multidimensional. It is not, however, magic. It can require creativity, and intuition, but it isn't some weird inexplicable superpower. It's not something that should be beyond the understanding, the aspiration or the interest of anybody. This diary is simply my best attempt at revealing what the process is like – a look under the hood. Wherever possible I will build what I say not around ethereal abstract nouns but around concrete examples, made of solid, earthbound words.

Every translator practises translation differently, and when talking about process I will of course only be speaking for myself, describing what seems to work for me. I will tell the truth about the things I find difficult, and the things I find easy. I will share examples from my very earliest drafts, however excruciating the idea of making these public may seem. I'll answer any questions you may have along the way, and I may well ask those of you reading to help me out with ideas when I get stuck.

Though I have read other things by Diamela, both in Spanish and in English translations, I know very little about this particular book. I've translated the first few pages already, and I'll talk about those soon, but most of the book will be entirely new to me. I tend to prefer to begin my translations like this, and to use the first draft as my process of discovery – the book's voice, plot, shape, language, pulse, everything will come into focus for me en route, as they do for any other first-time reader. By the time the English-language novel is fully formed, sometime in early April, it will have become temporarily the book I know best in the world, even if it's hard to imagine that now. My job, then, begins with a gradual process of falling in love with it; and then changing everything while also preserving its essence – but that sounds mysterious again, I know. So to put it another way: my job is to look closely at what the novel is currently doing – holding it up and turning it slowly so the light catches every syllable and comma – then to construct a new thing out of English words that holds as many of the same properties as I can manage. But truly it will seem less abstract as we progress – that process of construction is merely a long series of concrete choices, after all.

If you stick with this diary, you might discover that translation is more complicated than you imagined, or less; you may find it more interesting than you'd expected, or less. I won't give those guarantees. But I can promise that it will seem less mysterious, and I think that's important.

We begin, then, with my title. In English, the book will be called *Never the Fire Ever*.

At least, I think so. But – hmm – I might yet change my mind.

OK, I'll come back to that.

27 January

Love at First Sight?

Several kind comments on the blog, on Twitter and elsewhere, from those readers pleased to see the diary launched. Anne M., a fellow translator, remarked that she thinks the process of keeping this diary is "so brave", and when people say that, they usually mean "potentially very foolish", so if I wasn't worried about it before, I clearly ought to start worrying now...

She also picked up on my point about not having read the book in advance, writing:

> How do you know you'll fall in love with it if you've only read a few pages? Do you think your not-reading-the-book-before-you-start-translating-it method only works for short novels? Or only for very brave traductores?

Toby asked a related question on Twitter: I referred to gradually falling in love with the book during the translation process, but what happens, Toby asks, if I don't? And the answer, at least in part, is that you just persuade yourself temporarily that you do. You approach the book with something like devotion, with commitment, with generosity, with open-mindedness – what comes out of that attention is a kind of intimacy, at the very least. And that's close enough, I think.

Part of the answer to the questions about why I choose to do this also comes in a comment from Hilary (herself one of my favourite writers), who said: "I was surprised to hear that you don't read first, but of course, that makes sense. The original writer didn't read it first either" – yes, that's also absolutely at the heart of it, and that's at least a part of the pleasure. Doing my first draft totally fresh like this obviously more closely resembles the experience of any other reader discovering a book (I don't think you can ever replicate the particular electricity of a first encounter with a book, however good it might still be on multiple re-readings); but it's also got something of the experience of the writer discovering it in her first draft, too – trying to catch hold, keep hold of this thing while it's still moving, evolving, and that can be a thrilling ride. Or at least, here's hoping.

Anyway, here goes…

28 January

¡Chapter 1!

But, um, not actually chapter 1. I'm starting with chapter 2.
(Don't ask. I'll explain later.)
This is how it begins, in Diamela's words:[8]

Hace más de cien años que murió Franco. El tirano.
Profundamente histórico, Franco saqueó, ocupó, controló.
Fue, cómo no, coherente con el rol que hubo de representar.
Uno de los mejores actores para pensar la época. Anciano.
Militar. Condecorado por las instituciones. No brillante,
no, nunca, sino eficaz, obstinado, neutro. Necio, dices,
era necio. Ya ha transcurrido un siglo. No, no, me dices,
no un siglo, mucho más, más. Sí, te contesto, todo circula
de un cierto determinado modo, impreciso, nunca literal,
jamás.

And so, a first draft:

---

[8] If you don't know any Spanish, don't fret. I'll be including bits of Spanish throughout for anyone who might be interested in seeing it, but anything you actually need to know, I'll explain as we go.

*It's been more than a hundred years since Franco died
[rev?]. The tyrant. Deeply/Profoundly HISTORICO,
Franco SAQUEÓ, occupied, controlled. He was,
COMO NO, COHERENTE CON the role
he needed to represent [part he needed to play?].
One of the best actors for PENSAR the period/age.
ANCIANO. MILITAR. CONDECORADO
POR LAS INSTITUCIONES. Not brilliant [?],
no, never that, but EFICAZ, obstinate/stubborn,
neutral. NECIO, you say, he was NECIO. A century
has gone by already [It's been a century?]. No, no,
you say, not a century, much more, more. Yes, I answer
you, everything CIRCULA in a certain DETER-
MINADO [/certain?] way, IMPRECISO, never*
literal, never* [not ever?].*

The good news is that I've just done 100 words in
four minutes. Hooray for me.

The bad news is, well, obvious.

That little abomination is what my first drafts always
look like. I do them at pretty much my standard typing
speed, and while I try to be aware of potential problems
en route, I solve none of them. That will come later.

Eventually I'll decide whether to go for *Deeply* or
Profoundly, for *obstinate* or *stubborn*, based on what works
better to my ear once the rest of the sentence has cohered,
and on what I've learned about the voice. Most of the
words in Spanish are words whose regular meanings I
know, but I'm not sure how the author intends them or
what to do with them in English, and they can wait. So
although I do know what *saqueó* means, the English word
sacked isn't quite good enough and a better synonym
didn't come to me instantly, so I'll whizz past for now
and pop the right word in later.

For now, I just get any-old-rubbish on the page, and

note whatever I need to return to in drafts 2 to 99.

(Oh: *looted*. Yeah, it's obvious. "Franco looted, occupied, controlled." Or *plundered*. Actually either of those would do fine. Excellent.)

But let's take a look at that first sentence: you'll see I just went for "It's been more than a hundred years since Franco died", because there was a conversation in Chapter 1 in which a character asks when Franco died, so this line's a response, not just a statement out of the blue. I'm not sure about "It's" rather than "It is", but again, once I know the voice better, that sort of call will be more obvious. And I can tell already that I might reverse the ending of the sentence, so as to land on Franco's name: Spanish allows "since died <u>Franco</u>", which leads on to the second sentence – "The tyrant." – much more neatly. I can't use "since died Franco" myself, because that would be, you know, basically still Spanish; but I could perhaps end with "…since the death of <u>Franco. The tyrant.</u>" Yes, that's better. Remind me to change that, OK?

(Btw, you might have noticed – if you truly have nothing better to do – that in this sentence I've instinctively gone with *a hundred years* rather than <u>one</u> *hundred years*. Why? Because… I don't know. I might think about that later. *Cien años de soledad* is <u>One</u> *Hundred Years of Solitude* – how is this different?)

In one sense, or in *a* sense, these 15 lines are simple enough, inasmuch as they aren't full of words whose common meanings I don't know. In fact, the only thing I'll need to look up is *necio*, which typically means *foolish*, but which I know varies slightly in usage depending on where in the Spanish-speaking world we are, so I'm going to have to double-check specifically how the Chileans use it. (There are many, many things I don't know about my languages. I am, however, pretty good at knowing what I don't know, and that's vital.)[9]

Most of the things that I've left in Spanish in this instance, then, aren't cases where I need to know a word or phrase's dictionary meaning; rather they're cases where I need to figure out what this specific author means by them in this specific moment in this specific line. *Histórico* means *historic*, but in this sentence... huh? I need to decide whether in this context *eficaz* should be *effective* or *efficient* – any dictionary would tell you (reassuringly and unhelpfully) that it means both. English can be maddeningly demanding of precision.

When the narrator says Franco is "one of the best actors for *pensar* the age" – *pensar* meaning *to think* – so *one of the best actors for thinking the age...* You mean, for thinking *about*? For *us* to think about? *Who was best at* thinking about? What precisely is this simple word supposed to convey – or is the blurriness to the meaning deliberate (there are clearer ways of expressing this in Spanish), in which case should I retain it? That would cause its own problems.

I recently asked an author whether he'd used a certain word to mean X or Y, both of them plausible translations. He replied – I think trying to be helpful (I'm giving him the benefit of the doubt) – that "it's meant to be both". That, I pointed out to him politely, was every translator's least favourite answer. Retaining well-controlled ambiguity can be the hardest thing of all in a translation – more often than not, translators just need to make a choice. In this passage, "Anciano" and "Militar" are both adjectives (elderly, military); and they are both nouns (an old man, a soldier) – either pair could work in context, but in English, simply not choosing isn't an option.

---

[9] I translate from three languages, which between them are the biggest official languages in many dozens of countries. Occasional inadequacies in my levels of expertise are inevitable.

Well, it is for now, at least – thank god for first drafts! See you next week.

P.S. Oh – no – wait – it gets worse: in response to my introductory entry, there was a conversation on Twitter about how to translate the title – I'll write about that shortly. But that decision has just become more complicated, because the two different words the title uses for "never" also need to play against each other in the same way at the end of *this* passage – but what I want to do in this instance (*never, not ever*) won't match the working title. Oh, damn.

In short: don't be a translator. It's a very foolish thing to do. *Necio*!

(Being Spanish, should that be punctuated with an upside-down exclamation-mark at the start? Gah – I need to think of *everything*.)

29 January

An Interlude about Process

I feel as though my second long entry, with its four pages about all sorts of trivial word choices (and my failure to make them), will have driven away all but the bravest readers, so congratulations if you're still here.

As I explained, I like to do *very* quick first drafts, and then return to fix them, to fill in gaps and hone them, only after that first draft is done. What I did not go into is *why* I like to work like that, so before I go on, this is it…

Every translator's process will be different. I suspect one of the things that led me to mine was just a matter of personality, and taste. I could rationalise it in some cleverer way, develop some theoretical underpinning to justify it, but in truth it simply comes down to the fact that I am, I'm afraid, quite impatient. The idea of working on an exquisite first sentence slowly and diligently until I'm sure it's perfect and only then moving onto the second – as many translators do – to me that sounds frankly appalling. (As I'm sure my delinquent habits do to others.) All I want is to get something down, anything at all for now, keep moving, do the quantity first and deal with the quality later. Get from a blank page to some really bad draft first, and fast – and only then concentrate all my energy on making the really bad draft good, taking this wondrous and vibrant thing I've apparently killed, and by a laborious process of hyper-detailed surgery, coaxing it back to life.

My apparent haste at this stage in the process relates to something I've mentioned already, about liking to start translating a book without having read it first, so this quick first draft is also my first reading, and it's my discovery of what the book is. But it also relates to something else that's only personal – as it happens, I absolutely hate first-drafting, and I love editing my drafts. So I get the first bit over as quickly as I can, and weight my time as much as possible towards the kind of work I enjoy and I think I'm good at. (I often co-translate books with friends, and recently discovered that one of my co-translators particularly likes the first part of the process and doesn't much like the second, so we may finally have found the perfect Jack Sprat/wife arrangement.)

The other reason is to do with the working habits I've developed, and how the different bits of my working life fit together. Again, every translator's circumstances are different. But here's the thing: doing these quick first drafts in this way is *easy*. You're just skipping over the text, much as any semi-attentive reader might, and it doesn't require any great engagement at that stage. It doesn't require *getting into the zone*, or getting your ear attuned, or anything of that kind. If anything snags even for a moment, ignore its demands, just leave it and move on. This means that, unlike a lot of writing, it's a task that can be done despite distractions, it can be done in very brief fragments. When I'm working on a first draft, I can squeeze in two and a half minutes of easy work if I have three minutes between subway stops. I really can't do that with any other kind of writing, but this stage makes only the minimal demands on the brain. As somebody who travels a lot, this suits me. The most intense last stages of a book require a much deeper, more sustained engagement than I can get from just leaning on a bus stop for 45 seconds and knocking out a couple of quick rough sentences, but the first draft is totally, delightfully undemanding.[10]

This light-weight, low-engagement nature of these drafts makes them compatible not just with a pretty fragmentary working life – fitting in little bits between meetings, on trains, while waiting for people at cafés – but with other translation work, too. Three of the books I'm publishing this year all happen to be converging at proof-reading stage over the next fortnight (help!), and in these months when I'm translating Diamela's book I'm also going to have to read, write, and translate other little bits and pieces I've promised people. (Including some poetry. I normally know better than to agree to translate poetry, but I'm afraid I've lapsed, just this once, god help me…) It's a question of practicality: when you deliver a book to a publisher, you might then have six or eight months still to come of back-and-forth with an editor, a copy-editor, and then reading the proofs, so it's usually not feasible simply to wait till the entire process is over before starting the next project. (And it's not like I could handle doing exactly the same thing unchanging for long working day after day anyway. I'm very good at multitasking – I'm also incredibly bad at *not* multitasking. Too easily bored, too impatient.) But things like reading proofs of older books is quite compatible with writing first drafts of new ones – there's not much danger of

---

[10] Don't worry, I promise there will be plenty of proper agonising, rending of garments, etc., in the later stages. Something for you to look forward to.

interference of voice, rhythm, etc. because, well, there's not much care being given to the draft anyway. I'd find it hard to jump between, say, carefully reading final versions of different things – I'd worry about not being quite tuned in, it'd take a while to switch fully between them each time; but having different projects requiring quite different things of me in this way seems to work.

So I have various other bits of more demanding work scheduled for the next few weeks, while simultaneously I'm just blithely first-drafting this one without a care in the world. Then in the weeks that follow, when this book demands much more of my proper focus, and my carefully-tuned ear, and my problem-solving, and my judgment, then I'll give it much more exclusive attention. That's the difficult bit. To my mind, it's the fun bit, too.

30 January

Sabine has written in to say she feels that what I call my "really bad draft" of that early paragraph on the 28th does actually read well, for all the gaps, questions etc. And I do sort of know what she means. Obviously these first drafts are more problems than solutions, but I agree there are certain things that do come right even this early. One of the interesting collateral effects of working in this way – at speed, responding very immediately to the original as a reader – is that things like pacing (including sentence rhythm, punctuation) are often exactly right first time, as the draft just moves in sync with the original. Still got to get all the individual words right after that, of course. More on that tomorrow.

1 February

Frontists, Stalinists and Murderers

> *Frentista, estalinista, asesina loca. Una palabra detrás de otra, un conjunto de palabras elaboradas en una ecuación implacable. Sílabas sonoras, perfectas, que iban organizando una cadena armónica que resonaba igual que una recurrente letanía.*

So begins the next chapter, and I know it's going to cause me trouble. The first sentence is just four words:

Frentista, estalinista, asesina loca.

The first word, *Frentista*: this could be "Frontist", if we actually used such a word in English, which we don't. I believe (though will check) that it refers to a supporter of a specific *frente* (a political front), which in this case is a Chilean far-left revolutionary guerrilla movement. That means it's a word that will be familiar to the book's Chilean readers and carry with it a whole heap of powerful associations. But that is no use to most of my readers, clearly. If somebody called you a "frentista!" in Chile, that would have meant more than somebody yelling "hey, frontist!" at you in English, which just sounds silly. How, then, to convey what's required without any context?

The second word, *estalinista*: this simply means "Stalinist". We tend to capitalise such things in English more than they do in Spanish, but otherwise these words are a simple swap: estalinista => Stalinist. Hooray.

The third word, *asesina*: the word means murderer, killer, assassin (you can see the relation: *asesina, assassin*), but – this is important – referring unequivocally to a female killer, not a male one. We have *murderess* in English, I suppose, but that's not a word I'd choose to use if I can possibly avoid it. Besides I like the word "assassin", even if it's a bit weightier than "killer", not least because it would allow us then to keep many of the same sounds as the Spanish (estalinista asesina, Stalinist assassin) – but *assassiness* isn't a thing. (*Sassas… sassassiness…*? Nope, no idea.)

The fourth word, *loca*: this word means mad, crazy, and it, too, is in the feminine form, agreeing with *asesina*. It seems quite clear by the end of this little sentence that these three epithets are all referring to the same person, rather than a trio – a Frontist, a Stalinist and an assassin (walk into a bar?) – but because adjectives in Spanish usually follow nouns, having this "mad" at the end of the list means it could be attached either just to the last of the nouns or to *all* of them – so either she's a *Frontist (or whatever), a Stalinist, and a <u>mad</u> killer (woman)*, or *a <u>mad</u> Frontist (or whatever), Stalinist and killer (woman)*.

(Think about the equivalent in English, where one might put an adjective at the start of the list: if you decide to taste *green eggs and ham*, you know there's a chance the *green* could be referring to both foodstuffs, not just the first. If I tell you that "Outside my window I could see grey streets, cars and people" – can you be sure whether or not the cars and people are grey, too?[11])

Usually context offers some clues, but, being the start of a chapter, we go into this sentence without context, not even knowing who's being described. So... no help there.

Incidentally, neither *Frentista* nor *estalinista* are gender-specific, so give no indication of the gender of their subject; we only know it's a woman being described when we reach *asesina loca* (I'll write about this problem shortly). In English we could add a noun, some derogatory term that tends to be used for women: "Stalinist, murderer, mad commie cow/bitch"? It could also be e.g. "*murderous* bitch", or something, but I'm not sure calling someone murderous is the same as calling them an actual murderer, is it? Oh, and I know, *commie* isn't quite good enough for Frentista (supporter of the [insert specific name] Front), but you get the idea for now.[12]

One thing that has become very clear even in just the first few pages of the book is the density with which Diamela writes – it's not dense in the sense of being clogged or impenetrable, just in the economy with which so much happens in the language. Concision is so hard to retain in translation, and so far in this book there's no sprawling, there's no sagging, there are no extra words. So one of the things I'm going to have to do as I proceed is keep that totally disciplined tightness to my prose, too. The problem, though, is how do I do all the things she's doing in this sentence... in four words?

Incidentally, I do also have a clear sense from the Spanish of how I'd like that short sentence to *sound*, with

---

[11] A whole post on this single-adjective-multiple-nouns malarkey would follow on 9 March.

[12] For now! Everything about this draft is *for now*.

lots of echoing letters and syllables. (Try reading it aloud – even if you don't know any Spanish, it's a perfectly phonetically logical and regular language, so your guess will be pretty close.) But that awareness of the sound is not helped – nor is my mood – by the lines that follow that opening, describing it. Here, just in draft form:

> [Frentista, estalinista, asesina loca.] One word after another, a group of words developed into a relentless equation. Resonant, perfect syllables, organising a harmonic chain that rang out like a recurring litany.

Oh, *thanks*. No pressure, then.

P.S. Not all sentences are quite as troubling, or at least not at quite this problems-per-word ratio. If anybody has any clever solutions to this one, I will gladly split the 38p fee with you.

2 February

Déjà Vu

Though I only started my translation of this book in earnest last week, I actually translated the first chapter over a year ago.

That's not unusual. A translator might translate just an extract of a book to pitch it to a publisher, or as part of an audition process to be selected as the translator to win the contract, or in order to have a preliminary conversation about stylistic and editorial decisions with a co-translator or the editor-to-be. In my case, the chapter was for a funding application. As a result, though, while I'm first-drafting messily away and not doing any polishing till that draft is done, I do in fact have a reasonably clean opening 1500 words or so. I'll come back to them later, of course, and I suspect I'll change a lot based on what I'm yet to learn about what the author is up to, but I thought it might be nice to share a little of that slightly more polished work with you.

Having done this opening is instructive for me, too. Doing that one chapter with much more care than my usual first drafts allowed me to learn things about the intensity of the writing, about the rhythms and repetitions and the precisions of the writing, which will help me make my decisions as I go on. Well-written books teach you how to read them. How to translate them, too, I think.

So here is how (dedication and epigraph excepted) the book begins. Just ignore the asterisks – they indicate a recurring problem I'll write about next week...

> *We are lying in bed, surrendered★ to the legitimacy of a rest that we deserve. We are, yes, lying in the night, sharing. I feel your body folded up against my folded★ back. Perfect together. A curve is the shape that holds us best because we are able to harmonize and unmake our differences. My stature and yours, the weight, the arrangement of bones, of mouths. The pillow supports our heads in balance, separates our breathings. I cough. I lift my head from the pillow and lean my elbow on the bed so as to cough in peace★. It bothers you, my cough, and to some extent it worries you. Always. You move so as to let me know that you are there and that I have overdone it. But now you sleep while I remain ritually wakeful and drowning. I will have to tell you, tomorrow, yes, it really will be tomorrow that I'm going to have to ration your cigarettes, to restrict them greatly or stop buying them altogether. We can't stretch to them. You'll clench your jaw and you'll close your eyes when you hear me and you won't answer me, I know it. You'll remain unfazed as if my words were totally unfounded and the pack I faithfully buy you was still there, full.*
>
> *You like it, you think it's important, you need to smoke, I know it, but you can't anymore, I can't, I don't want to. Not anymore. You'll think, I know it, about how much you've kept yourself going on the cigarettes you systematically consume. That's how it has been, but it is no longer necessary.*

It's not.

No, I can't sleep and between the minutes, through the seconds I can't seem to specify, a worry inserts itself that is absurd but which asserts itself as decisive, death, yes, the death of Franco. I can't remember when Franco died. When it was, what year, what month, in what circumstances, you told me: Franco's died, he finally died lying there like a dog. But you were smoking and so was I at the time. You were smoking as you talked about death and I was smoking and while all my attention was on your teenaged face, openly resentful and lucid and also somehow dazzling, I stubbed out my cigarette understanding that it was the last, that I wouldn't do it ever again, that I never really liked to inhale that smoke and swallow the burning of the paper. I feel your elbow resting against my rib, I think about how I still have my rib and I accept, yes, I surrender to your elbow and I resign myself to my rib.

I turn, put my hand on your hip and I shake you once, twice, fast, obvious. When did Franco die, I ask you, what year. What, you say, what? When did he die, I say, Franco, what year. With a single impulse you sit up in bed, quickly, filled with a muscular rage you never practise anymore and which surprises me. You lean your head against the wall, but immediately slip down between the sheets again to turn your back on me.

When, I ask you, when?

With your breathing too agitated, you move towards the edge of the bed, I don't know, you answer me, be quiet, go to sleep, turn round. A precise day of a precise year but which is no part of any order. A scene that's detached, inarticulate now, in which we smoked, concentrated, dedicated to our very first cell, while you, precociously wise, with the fullness that talent can allow, you maintained a few legitimate, coherent words that

couldn't be ignored and we looked enraptured at you –
your arguments – as you explained the death of Franco
and I, transfixed by the harshness of your words, put out
my cigarette possessed by a final disgust and watched
the paper crushed against the filter, looked at it in the
ashtray and thought, never again, that's the last one, it's
over, I thought and I thought why had I smoked so much
that year if I didn't even like the smoke, not really. I can
picture the ashtray, the stubbed-out cigarette with the
scant strings of tobacco loose at its centre. I have got that.
I have also got the death of Franco, but not the year, nor
the month let alone the day. Tell me, tell me, I ask you.
Don't start, don't keep on, go to sleep, you answer. But
I can't, I don't know how to sleep without retrieving the
lost plot, without dodging the terrible blank in time that
I need to attract. The end of the cigarette crushed against
the ashtray, my fingers, the sequence of your convincing
words, lying there like a dog, in his bed, the killer or
maybe you said: the murderer and my final disgust at
that mouthful of smoke, the last one.

The public death of Franco, lying in bed, dying of
everything, practically without any organs, you said, the
tyrant, you were saying, dead of old age or of ancient
age, surrounded by his entourage, you were saying, by
Francoists, doctors. At night, late, at the edge of a thor-
ough dawn the discussions continued, the arguments,
and among all the possible words, of course, yours were
the ones that sounded most expert or most correct, while
I smoked right through that night that never wavered
until, all of a sudden, I felt truly acidic, my lungs, and I
had to put it out, that cigarette, for ever.

That's about half of the first chapter. You can now see
what Franco was doing in chapter 2. I'll explain those
asterisked problems next week.

4 February

Suggestions

Several people have written with suggestions for the sentence I was grappling with on Monday.

A fellow Spanish translator, Daniel S., wrote:

Regarding Frentista, I think Diamela may be referring to "Frente Patriótico Manuel Rodríguez", essentially a Marxist-Leninist guerrilla fighting against Pinochet. Of course, most Anglo (and, indeed, non-Chilean) readers will be oblivious to the context. "Paramilitary" might be another choice, but the word is just too bulky (even in Spanish, it's abbreviated to "Paracos"). Instead, why not use a slur to which the Anglo world has a lot of exposure, such as "terrorist"? It carries the harsh edge that Frentista likely did for the Chileans in that fraught decade. "Lefty" could also strike the right tone, but isn't vicious enough. I also think you can turn "Murderess" into "Murderous" in the adjective form. In my mind, the best solution is something along these lines: "Terrorist. Stalinist. Murderous bitch."

Yes, that's the Frente I'm assuming Diamela's referring to. *Paramilitary* conveys useful information, but I agree the tone is wrong. It might be that the solution is not one word, but two – not to just call them *lefties* or *commies* but *lefty/commie thugs* or similar.

One of the difficulties (as so often) is coming up with something that is helpfully familiar to the reader, so they understand the weight of what you're talking about, but also which isn't loaded with associations that are in fact *un*-helpful, and potentially distracting. That's the problem, perhaps, with *terrorist* – is this the sort of person an Anglo reader would think of when they hear that word? Not sure.

Lara suggested:

> *Could you use "Guerrilla" for "frentista"? That doesn't do much to solve the "loca" problem, but it's evocative, totally intelligible for English readers, and preserves the feel & sound of Spanish. Plus, the juxtaposition with "Stalinist" goes some ways towards situating her politically, which relieves you of using a word like "commie", no? When you find out which "frente" she belonged to, you could potentially add its name/acronym before "guerrilla" (e.g., "FPMR guerrilla")? Is the frente described in the ensuing chapter? At what point does one start using endnotes, in these cases?*
>
> *As for the "loca"… I like the punchiness of "bitch" here, and it lands well at the end of the sentence in the same way that "loca" does in Spanish, but the meaning isn't quite the same… What about "unhinged"? That works well at the beginning of the sentence, which allows you to preserve the ambiguity of the original. So… "Unhinged assassin, guerrilla, Stalinist bitch"? Or is that too much?*

Yes, "guerrilla" is definitely a possibility. The problem with putting the acronym/name before it is that while it helps the reader with an informational gloss, it sounds very much less like an insult somebody would actually use.

And yes, "bitch" or similar would be replacing "loca", or rather it would be replacing the component of "loca" that reveals the gender of the person being insulted, but there'd still have to be a "mad" somewhere or other, too. "Unhinged" is a great word, but again, as with the acronym above, I feel I need to create the sort of insult that one might spit out at somebody. "Mad commie bitch!" is too much the other way, but has the benefit of being plausible as a bitterly spat insult. Tricky, this business, isn't it?

8 February

Why Tired Narrators Are Annoying[13]

Imagine a novel that began, in French, with the narrator writing the simple sentence "Je suis fatigué." Or "Estoy cansado," in Spanish.

If you happen not to know either of these languages, the totally straightforward translation would be "I'm tired."

But there's a problem. (Well, of course there is.)

Since every language works differently, every language encodes slightly different information into its words, beyond their simple meaning. In this case, the word "fatigué" (or "cansado") tells you not only that the speaker is tired, but that the speaker is tired *and male*. Because adjectives agree with their nouns in all the languages I translate from, a first-person narrator often testifies to their gender over and over, in a way that's totally inconspicuous to the reader. My English opening line "I'm tired" does no such thing.

---

[13] When I wrote this entry for the blog, somebody I'm not going to name (but it was Sam) accidentally published it with the title "Why Tired Translators Are Annoying". Yeah, "accidentally".

I've read so many English translations where a discrepancy has slipped in – where there is nothing in the translation to confirm how the narrator identifies their gender for many pages (or chapters), but where I know the original reader could have been left in no doubt. As a reader of an English novel that begins "I'm really tired today," you either unconsciously make an assumption about who's talking to you, or you consciously take a guess – and you might discover 25 pages later that you've been reading it all wrong. That's not to say that the doubt can't be effective in some ways, but it's certainly not what this particular book intended.

(Of course, the converse is also true. I know two very good English-language novels published last year, both written in the first person, in which the respective narrators choose not to identify their gender, and it would be all but impossible to translate that effect into, for instance, a Romance language, in which every adjective betrays more information than in English; or into Russian, say, where verbs in the past tense reveal their subject's genders, too.)

Needless to say, I've come up against this problem in Diamela's book countless times already.

Wherever it's an issue, I need to find some way of having my tired character say the equivalent of "I'm tired (*and btw male*)." That bit in parentheses doesn't look like it's in the two-word original, but of course it is – it's just encoded in the word for "tired" rather than a separate unit. I'm adding words, but conveying precisely the same information.

Similarly, just as in English we can choose to differentiate between an "actress" and an "actor" if we need to, different languages have the option of gendering nouns like doctor, teacher, nurse, or – as you saw a couple of entries ago – assassin. You might assume the relevant character's gender based on whatever prejudices you have, but – unlike in

Spanish etc. – it's not always 100% confirmed. If you come up with any clever solutions to this problem, please feel free to give me one. *As the actress said to the bishop* being one of those lines where you probably assumed on balance of probability that the bishop was a man, but she needn't be.[14]

A few problems of this kind that I've come across recently:

"The doctor sighed and stood up."
"I've always been a big fan of black and white movies…"
"People tell me I'm pretty funny, actually."

What I did about them:

"The doctor sighed and got to her feet."
"Ever since I was a boy, I've always liked black and white movies."
"People tell me I'm a pretty funny guy, actually."

If you'd read my translations containing those last three lines, I doubt you'd have noticed I had smuggled in that extra information (unlike if I'd said "The doctor, who in this instance was *a woman*, sighed and stood up"), so the significant information is conveyed to you just as inconspicuously as it is in the original.

I've just raced through a new chapter of Diamela's book whose very first sentence has the narrator describing themselves as feeling *contaminada* – that is to say, *polluted + female*. I hope that by this point in the book it will have become clear to my readers that there is one consistent narrator, so I can ignore the problem here so long as I've established that she is a woman before now. And indeed, the Spanish reader would have been in no doubt from the very first page.

---

[14] Worth noting that the U.S. equivalent phrase – "That's what she said…" – leaves no such room for ambiguity.

Look again at those opening lines, from the draft I shared with you a few days ago:

We are lying in bed, surrendered* to the legitimacy of a rest that we deserve. We are, yes, lying in the night, sharing. I feel your body folded up against my folded* back. Perfect together. A curve is the shape that holds us best because we are able to harmonize and unmake our differences. My stature and yours, the weight, the arrangement of bones, of mouths. The pillow supports our heads in balance, separates our breathings. I cough. I lift my head from the pillow and lean my elbow on the bed so as to cough in peace*.

That first asterisk relates to the Spanish word *entregados*, which tells you that of the people who have surrendered, at least one of them is male. (I'll come back to this in a sec.) The third asterisk tells you that the person who is trying to cough in peace – *tranquila* – is a woman. As the translation stands, you might make a guess to that effect, but there's some information that was in the Spanish that's still missing here.

(Obviously I'm using gendered language as an example here, but all translation involves figuring out what is being conveyed within words – beyond only meanings – and then mapping it onto another language that might be more or less resistant.)

To understand what's happening in that first asterisk, you just need to know that Spanish uses the masculine as the default (this is quite common in languages, or indeed not in languages) – so as long as there's just one male, it trumps any number of females. In other words:

- *Cansado* – singular, male;
- *Cansada* – singular, female;
- *Cansados* – plural, male; or a mixed group even if it's 99 women and one man;
- *Cansadas* – plural, female.

(Similarly you have a sister – *una hermana*; or a brother – *un hermano*. But if you have 99 sisters and one brother, your siblings are still your *hermanos*.)

Hence that first adjective (*entregados*) tells us that the people who've surrendered are plural (it becomes clear in the next line that there are specifically two of them, not more), and that at least one of them is male. Half a dozen lines later, the narrator identifies herself as female (*tranquila*). Less than a hundred words into the book, any possible doubt or ambiguity about the gender of the two lead characters has been resolved.

So, yes, at present the English is lacking some vital certainty. One more for the ever-growing list of things-to-figure-out-at-some-point.

Oh – just one last pleasing little thing. Have a look at that sentence with the second asterisk:

I feel your body folded up against my folded back.

In the Spanish, the first "folded" is *doblado*, the second is *doblada*. The slight difference is because one is describing a body (*cuerpo*, a masculine noun), and the second a back (*espalda*, a feminine noun). Neither adjective, strictly speaking, is describing the person – that's not why they're gendered as they are – but it does at least give a nice little suggestion of who is who. We meet the man with his *doblado* body, the woman with her *doblada* back. It's a nifty little trick, I think.

(So long as you're not trying to translate it, of course, in which case it's still brilliant but also simultaneously a bit of a nightmare. Good writers can be really annoying like that.[15])

[15] If any of my writers are reading this, I'm OBVIOUSLY not talking about you. Only the other ones. You aren't annoying *at all*.

54

8 February (2)

Hot on the heels of that last post about inflected adjectives (adjectives that adjust slightly to match the noun they're describing), this message has come in from my friend Vineet:

Gosh, such a tricky subject (and I empathise). As a translator from French, I come across this all the time – this and the perennial chestnut of "tu" versus "vous". In many ways – not wishing to sound defeatist – the tu/vous distinction is one that I've now learnt just to live with, in as much as elegant solutions to the problem are hard to find. And the issue of inflected adjectives reflecting gender sometimes veers in that direction (I find) because the insertion of a "btw I'm male/female" can end up being so intrusive, or so hard to insert with stealth, that in the cost/benefit analysis it's not worth doing. I guess it's the kind of calculation that transla-tors make every five minutes. I looked back at a recent novel with a similar challenge in the opening chapter, where the gender is revealed by the word "nourrie" (as in "breastfed"). The French reader knows at once that we are talking about a little girl. In my translation I glided over this one – leaving it as "breastfed" – as, helpfully, the narrator herself states, barely half a page later, that she is now a "little girl of five" or similar. So I just let the English reader wait a tad longer than the French one to find out. That said, the book itself was called The Woman Who Didn't Grow Old, and the entire thing is in the first person, so although not a given, I'd suggest that any reader picking it up is going to assume it's a female voice.

Decisions, decisions. I sometimes think that's what I should be – a "decider", not a "translator". ("Decider" being uninflected in English, as you'll know.)

Yes, everything is case-by-case, and in the example Vineet mentions, if the English naturally has the reveal only half a page later, that doesn't seem a problem – better in that instance to have a very slight lag than trying to shoehorn in some extra information to correspond to the moment the French reader would get it – seems like the right call. But as he says, in our role as deciders/decidresses,[16] we're having to make versions of this calculation all the time.

Oh, and having made a fuss about the way gendered adjectives are problematic, I've just run into the Spanish adjective "imperturbable" which is causing me problems because it's *not* gendered. Honestly, there's no pleasing some people.

---

[16] Microsoft Word is clearly not keen on gendering nouns either, and wants to know whether perhaps I'm writing about "desi dresses"?

12 February

To the, or…

One of the most common words in my first drafts is "[the]".

Not "the", you understand, but "[the]". Each time it appears, it's telling me that there's a definite article in the original, but that I don't know what to do about it. As I imagine has become clear to you by now, my first drafts are all about deferring decisions, and this is one of the regular troublemakers.

In one sense, this should of course be easiest of words to translate: *a*, *o*, *as* and *os* are all Portuguese words that mean *the* in English. Just as *la*, *le* and *les* do in French; and *la*, *el*, *las*, *los* in Spanish. But anybody who's ever moved between two languages will know that they aren't precisely equivalent sets of words, matching like for like, but whole systems that operate quite differently. Knowing how to translate a word as simple as a definite article doesn't mean merely knowing what a definite article looks like in the other language and replacing it with your own definite article; more than that, it requires knowing how that other language actually *uses* them.

And Spanish – like Portuguese, like French – uses them quite differently from English. Just because.

In very brief: these languages use all definite articles in the same places where we use them in English; but they also use them in places where we don't. So a definite article in that other language might indicate the need for one in English; or alternatively it might indicate no such thing.

(The opposite is true in a language like Russian, which doesn't have articles at all, so the absence of one could suggest the absence of one in English. Or, again, you know, *not*.)

"I like ice cream", rendered into some of those Romance languages, becomes "*I like the ice cream*"; whereas the English "I like the ice cream", well, that would be – ah, OK, that's "*I like the ice cream*", too. So when a definite article appears in a piece of writing in one of those languages, how is a poor translator to know which it is? If it's not totally clear, a normal reader can slip over it, not snagging on the slight ambiguity (what a luxury to be a normal reader!), but the translator needs actively to choose. Is this character really saying that they like chips, or that they like the chips?

Context often tells you a lot, of course. If the preceding question was "What's your favourite food?", the answer is probably "I like chips". If a child is being asked "What do you think of this lovely meal granny has prepared for you?", the answer is probably "I like the chips". (Unless the meal in question doesn't involve any chips, and the child is being petulant, in which case "*I like chips*" will probably do it.)

On page 18 of this novel, there's a classic case, for which my current translation reads "[The] rice goes well with [the] bread." Either a general statement, then, or an observation about a specific meal. In this case, when

I come to the second draft, it'll likely be obvious – the characters are having dinner, and (probably) that's what the narrator is referring to.

The fact I haven't yet had my lunch might explain why I do seem to be tending towards the food examples.

In the opening section of the book, the part I quoted at length last week, there's a moment when these characters are either *talking about death*, in abstraction, or *talking about the death* – because a specific death, Franco's, has just been mentioned. In theory it could be either, but in English it makes a difference, and so based on various factors (context, characters, probability), I need to make a decision. To *the*, or not to *the*?[17]

This discrepancy in how articles get used is an example – a pretty obvious one – of how languages function differently. But I'm mentioning it because I hope it'll illustrate something of the process I've been describing, too. While my hurtling first draft really doesn't slow down to make decisions of this kind, that doesn't mean it's totally inattentive, because while I don't need to solve problems, I do need to know they're there. So long as I remain alert to problems as I read, and especially alert to ambiguities, this should stop me from making any decisions inadvertently. (In another book, a character introduced a young man as her "boyfriend" or as her "fiancé", depending. The first draft didn't just plump for whichever came to me first, it said "This is my boyfriend/fiancé", so I knew there was a decision that needed confronting at some point, and I wouldn't accidentally miss it.)

The first draft, then, doesn't just allow for doubt, it tunes into it, it positively encourages it. It just makes sure every possible doubt is left unresolved but recorded.

---

[17] And no, this entire entry wasn't just so I could make that joke – honest.

Today's draft pages include:

- "They were talking/chatting"
- "I look at you from the edge of the bed and I have doubts/I hesitate."
- "but seemed surprisingly resistant/hardy"
- "I could see it in his/her/your eyes"
- (and obviously a lot of [the]s)

In each case, a little ambiguity flared up along my way, and I had to be sufficiently alert so as to avoid inadvertently shutting down any possibilities too early; so I registered it, just enough to put a pin in it before racing on.

13 February

I've just received a message from Anne R., who quotes from my entry of January 28th, in which I wrote: "I've instinctively gone with *a hundred years* rather than *one hundred years*. Why? Because... I don't know." Anne responds:

> *Of course you do. It's rhythm. You're retaining the rhythm of the Spanish here, and in One Hundred Years of Solitude the title replicates the strong initial stress by using One instead of A.*

Yeah, Anne's right, of course rhythm is a big part of it. And examining the workings of the line will reveal that. When I say I don't know, I guess what I really meant was that I don't stop to think about it – I go with what feels right, and while I probably *could* explain the decision if I chose to turn back and look at it, most of the time I don't allow it any such deliberate intention.

Anne makes the point, also, that "All writing is translation, in a sense...", and yes, it's true that what I've just said is like most kinds of writing, of course. (Anne is a writer herself.) The fact that you don't think about your choice of word A rather than word B doesn't mean the choice is irrelevant, but only that it doesn't always require deliberate intent, weighing up pros and cons for each word and comma – I know when the rhythm is just right even without counting syllables. One of the curiosities of this diary is that it requires examining and articulating a process that so often happens almost entirely by instinct. What I don't yet know is whether that examination/ articulation will make the choices any more deliberate and might therefore actually change the translation itself. We shall see…

14 February

Distractions

Nothing at all is going to be happening to my translation this week. And so I will have nothing to report.

I've got proofs for a couple of other books to sign off, and two other short translations to get done, and a couple of project proposals, and a lot of meetings, ~~and a promising new Netflix series to watch~~, so I know I won't get a chance to work on Diamela's novel for a bit.

I suppose I could pretend I'm still doing it, and just write a couple of entries about translationy things in very general terms, but, well, I did say in my introduction that I would tell you the truth, and the truth is that you don't always get to focus on one main project uninterrupted, and sometimes things get in the way, and I'm afraid that's the sort of week this is going to be. Such is the freelance life!

But I'm still well on course to hit the targets on my schedule, so I can afford a week of other work distractions without fretting too much. I'll be back to this book next Monday and will resume the diary then with a status report.

Have a good week!

21 February

Back to the Book

Well, I'm back, after a week being kept busy on other projects.

I'm not going to report back in any detail on the other stuff I was working on, as I really do want this diary to be about the specific book and documenting the process of its translation, rather than general musings about the translator's life, which I think would be *even more* self-indulgent. All I will say, then, is that in addition to reading proofs etc., I did spend some of the week doing some other translating, and at least a part of it was working on a small collection of poems, and that – contrary to all expectations and my usual mild allergy to translating poetry – I did in fact survive the experience. So here I am again.

Back at the first draft. What with other assorted distractions, my aim is to get it finished by about March 8th, a couple of weeks from now. (Remember that I'm racing through without doing any of the hard bits, and also that the book is very short. The full novel will come to something like 30,000 words.[18] To give you a sense of what that means: if you've been reading this diary, you'll have read 9,750 words of my ramblings already.)

When I returned to the drafting this morning after a week away, I recognised a phenomenon that always hits me around this stage in the first draft. Two things happen simultaneously, seemingly in a tussle with each other: I start really hating the process, and I start really loving the book.

I mentioned at the start of this diary that I was embarking on this novel without having read much of it – and the reassuring news is, well, wow, it's *really* good. When we get to later stages in the process and I have some more polished work to share with you, I hope you'll see why – it's mesmerising. I'm totally engrossed in the rhythms of this voice, and the detail. But at the same time, the longer I'm at first-draft stage and the more aware I am of how beautifully Diamela's original book seems to be developing before my eyes, the bigger the gap between the two seems to become, and more impatient I get at this process I'm engaged in. It feels like translating is just slowing down the thing I want to do which is simply read the book at pace and take all the stimulation it offers and not worry about anything else.

So I really want the first draft to be *over*. Then I can start the detailed work of moulding it into something that I hope will be just as mesmerising in English as the Spanish is proving to be. At the moment I'm just hacking bits of rock that are *very approximately* the right size out of the quarry, and no one ever became a sculptor in order to do that bit – all the real artistry of shaping it is yet to come, and for me, the finer the work, and the closer it gets to being tinkered into finished form, well, the happier I am working on it.

---

[18]   *Oh, how wrong you were. (Ed.)*

Which is to say: I'm going to be grumpy for a couple of weeks. I need to remind myself that then the fun begins, of course – but in the meantime, I'm producing stuff like this:

I could say now that an [some?] organic reason IMPULSÓ [impelled?] me. I was carrying within my body a biological MALESTAR that INCITÓ [or impelled here?] me to PROMOVER the first crisis. I don't remember/cannot recall my pain, I don't know which organ, which point on/in the body. Later, when the meeting/encounter was finished, I fell into a state of ESTUPOR. But you [tú], the SECRE-TARIO, the MAS HABILITADO of us, did not express a trace of disgust/distaste [trace of distaste ?? X], you answered serenely and managed, in a way, to re-establish [an?] equilibrium [/balance]. Years later, when the unknowns [/the mysteries?] between us had already been brought/knocked down, I understood that you had acted [no – presumably that I had acted?] COMO UNA PARTE TUYO, that it was you who had [you were the one who had?] pushed me in some mysterious way to produce the [that?] disturbance, [that thing] which you so needed [in order] to validate your PRECISIÓN [?].

You'd be hard pressed to recognise with any confidence that we're talking about a great novel – or indeed that translation is a delightful process – from those words. But I know it's the price to pay. The first draft sets up all the rest.

This is also, it must be said, where the impostor syndrome tends to kick in. I'm pretty happy editing my work, taking something bad and making it better, but until I can get down to doing that, I'm just running on faith. This is going to be good? Ever? *Really?* Seems unlikely…

Ugh, such a long way to go.

In the meantime, I mentioned in response to some conversations on Twitter that I'd write about why the title was causing trouble, too, so I'll do that in the next entry, to take my mind off the ENDLESS AND ANNOYING first draft.

24 February

Never Again?

It often happens that titles change as a book moves between its first incarnation and its rebirth in a new language. Titles can be among the hardest things to translate, not least because they're often doing a great deal, very economically. You have one word, or a couple, or maybe as many as half a dozen, which have to sound good and intriguing (titles, like jacket designs, are part of the publisher's marketing proposition just as much as they're a part of the writer's work of art), there might cleverly be a couple of different ways of reading this title, it should tell you something about the book (a steer to the reader about what aspect is especially important), and so on. Finding the right formulation to do all those things concisely is hard enough in just one language, let alone in a way that can work identically well in more than one. So, as I said, they sometimes have to change.

(Only last week I was involved in a long e-mail debate with an author, editor and publisher trying to find a new title for a novel that we hoped would do everything each of us wanted perfectly. We failed, obviously.)

For Diamela's book, I've not had any conversation with the publishers in which the possibility of completely changing the title has come up, nor have I mooted it with Diamela herself, so I'm assuming that – hoping that – we're going to aim to make a close English version of the original title work. That original, as I mentioned way back in the first entry, is

Jamás el fuego nunca

So, middle things first: *el fuego* means "the fire". That part at least is weirdly easy. Even the definite article! But now what?

Well, *Jamás* means "never".

And *nunca* means "never".

And so you can see, right away, my first problem.

There's not a huge amount of clear blue water between the two words in Spanish, but the usage is slightly different; the important thing for you to know is that basically the former sounds a bit more emphatic than the latter – and yet "never" is the English word that would come most readily to hand in both cases.

Our working title has always been *Never the Fire Ever*, and I like the sound of that – I like those bookending rhymes (which aren't in the Spanish), and the *Ever* at the end does, to my ear, work as a reinforcing extra negative. But I'm faintly bothered that it's a bit more, well, *normal* than the Spanish – not the whole phrase, but we do use "never… ever" for emphasis quite commonly in English. And I also know that if the words *Jamás* and *Nunca* are in the title like this, a reader is certainly going to notice when they crop up in the text (as happened at the end of the little extract I quoted on January 28), so I must keep in mind that whatever I do with the title will inevitably have implications for things that happen later.

(For one book I worked on many years ago, the publisher kept changing their mind about the title, and each time they did, I had to rewrite the last paragraph of the book. Let's not do that again.)

That bit I quoted in the earlier entry threw up the possibility of something like _Not Ever the Fire Ever_, which is weird in a way I rather like. Or _Not Ever the Fire, Ever_ with a comma? Though this does now make me think of the "Charlie & Lola" picture book, _I Will Not Ever Never Eat a Tomato_, which it probably shouldn't. (Don't get me wrong. I adore Lauren Child's books. But they are absolutely not in any way a remotely suitable or helpful echo in this instance.)

All of which would probably be solvable, except that the big problem is still ahead. As @siellosvieran pointed out on Twitter when I started the diary, the title is a line from a César Vallejo poem. And so in theory – everything, fortunately, is still only in the realm of theory at this point – the title should be translated in such a way that it could be made to work within that same context, as if extracted from an English translation of the Vallejo poem. In an alternative reality, I could, of course, just decide that the origins of the line are irrelevant and I don't care and I'll ignore the poem and just translate the title as a title. Except that the Vallejo poem quotation _is the book's epigraph_.

Tsk.

Sure, I could find an existing translation of the Vallejo poem and pull the line out of that – that'd be easy enough – but what are the odds that whatever was used in those translations would stand alone as a good title? (Zero. The odds are zero. In case my rhetorical question wasn't sufficiently obvious.)

Here, then, is the epigraph, which gives the title just a little more poetic context:

> *jamás el fuego nunca*
> *jugó mejor su rol de frío muerto.*

(It's not the start of a sentence – it comes at the end of a series of "Jamás…" lines.)

The first few Google hits on existing translations offer me:

> *never did the fire/play better its role of dead coldness!*
> *never, the fire never/acted better its role of cold death!*
> *never did the fire ever/play better its role of dead cold!*★
> *never did the fire ever/play deadlier its roll of cold death!*

These are mostly not good. The one with the asterisk kind of works, and I think is the closest to how I'd do it myself, but that's still not much use to me. If you don't understand Spanish, you'll at least have a sense of the meaning of the lines – and my new verb problem. If I'm thinking about the poetic context (as the epigraph requires that I do), I won't be able to make that line work as any variation on "Never the fire ever/did such-and-such…"; English expects the verb *did* up-front – "Never *did* the fire do such-and-such…" – if it is to retain the naturalness of the Spanish. (Because although that first line of the epigraph, and therefore the title, sound curious in isolation, the second half normalises the first.)

So – options?

Well, I could still just pretend I haven't noticed the epigraph. Make a title that works really well as a title and plead ignorance about everything else. (Remind me not to mention this idea in public.) Otherwise I need to figure out a translation that works for the epigraph – that is to say, for that *pair* of lines – but a part of which also makes me happy enough as a title.

For example… how about privileging the poem, and so calling the book *Never Did the Fire*? The epigraph could have both nevers – <u>Never</u> *did the fire* <u>ever</u> *play better etc.* – but they are no longer both in the title. Maybe that's OK, maybe that never–never emphasis isn't the most important thing? And this title does have that lovely sense of *incompleteness* that the Spanish has, which the epigraph then serves somehow to make sense of.

I suppose in theory the title could then also be the whole *Never Did the Fire Ever*, but, well, no. (Apart from everything else, putting the verb in there now sounds too much like "Never have I ever", a game that's about as relevant to this book as Lauren Child is. "Never did the fire ever go skinny-dipping", etc.) But curtailing it after the fourth word – *Never Did the Fire* – hmm, it's not an obvious title but the more I look at it… you know, I actually quite like that.

I'm honestly a little surprised, as I always mean to use these entries to lay out insoluble-seeming problems, I never actually expect (ever, not ever) to find solutions along the way. Not that we won't come back to it later, and it'll need approval from publishers and author and everyone else, but as a new working title, yeah – it'll do. That feels like progress!

How weird!

Anyway, more on my translation of *Never Did the Fire* next week.

3 March

Something for the Weekend

Well, I seem to have slowed down.

Not because I have a lot of other things distracting me this week – I don't, no more than usual – but because apparently I have simply run out of steam. I know that I only need a few more days' sprint and I'll be done with the first draft – cannot wait till that moment comes – but it's just been really *slow going*.

I'm not even sure why, to be honest. I suspect it's partly just a question of mood (it has come to my notice that not everything in the wider world is going totally optimally in every respect right now, which is obviously something of a disappointment...), and as I've said before, this part of the process is *always* the one I like least. In combination, these things have meant a week or so of incredibly sluggish progress.

When the first lockdown happened last year, it almost completely removed my ability to focus on reading for any length of time – I didn't read a book for about three months (and, in some ways more worryingly, I didn't even especially miss it until quite late on); but I was lucky that at least translating, for me, was largely unaffected. The total devastation of my reading attention-span didn't affect the work, which just filled all the empty space created by the inability to read (and to travel, to have a normal life, etc.). The work, as long as I could do it, was helpfully escapist. Not this week, though. This week I've found myself getting distracted after just twenty-minute bursts – and, given the way I work, it's hard to make progress that way. I really need to get my head down and just power through it – the reward waiting for me at the end will be the really fun part of the job – but it's not easy.

The fact that the book itself is a difficult one probably doesn't help, either, of course. If you've been following this diary, you'll know that I do this draft quickly (OK, *in theory*), deferring anything that I don't instantly know how to deal with. Well, this book has a much higher Parts-I-haven't-solved quotient than most, making it harder both to anticipate the pleasure in what the translation will eventually (I hope) become, and also to get any kind of momentum. In other books, racing through a sentence and just dropping in a provisional Spanish noun every few lines still feels like there's some real pace to what you're doing and it can even be, almost, enjoyable (for the part of your brain that's discovering a great novel as you read); whereas having to copy out several bits of Spanish on every line, little three- or four-word clusters where I just can't see at first glance which word is supposed to refer to what, well, that just feels less like pleasure-reading and more like wading in heavy boots through deep, thick mud.

I remember my friend Nick describing multiple readings of the same book by comparison to the experience of being in a new town and walking the same route several times over: the first time, you're sort of focusing on "How do I get there?", but once you *know* how you get there, you start being able to focus on lovely little details along the way – once you know your route, you don't have to worry about "Is this where I turn left?", you can take in the view. It's only just occurred to me that I might think of translation in these terms – right now I'm just trying to get from A to B, whatever it takes, with no thought to anything but arriving safely at my destination. (The terminal phrase I'm heading for is "… because, after all, we no longer have anything to lose", on page 166 of Diamela's original, and that'll be the sign that I've made it.) In a week or two, I'll be back at the beginning, but with the route fully charted out, and I can start noticing the elaborate doorways and shop signs and manhole covers and partly erased graffiti and gargoyles. That collection of details is what makes the spirit of the place, of course, not the set of from-A-to-B directions.

Hmm. I might take the weekend off, do other bits of work in the meantime (I might even read a book!), and return to this draft on Monday, and take a run at it.

Though it doesn't often feel like it, I do know in my brain that the end of draft 1 isn't far away. Then I can turn to the fun bit, which is good news for me; and it's definitely *great* news for you because then I'll also be able to stop the self-indulgent grumbling and go back to writing about verbs and ambiguity and commas and stuff. Something for us all to look forward to.

P.S. Current (slightly amended) plan: complete draft by Friday March 12th; one clear month to revise and revise and revise, and deliver to publishers on the 12th of April.[19] That's about a week after I'd originally hoped to be done, so I should try not to slip any further. But let's see how next week goes…

---

[19] LOL. *(Ed.)*

9 March

A Hopefully Interesting, Long, Slightly Tricky, Detailed Diary Entry

I presume everyone reading this has received those e-mails purporting to come from a good friend of yours, which say something like: "Hello Dear! I saw this SECRET video of you and couldn't believe my eyes!! MUST watch here: www.... xxxxxxxx"

When you received it, I hope you did not click on the link. Because whatever the sender name might have suggested, this delightfully inviting message did not in fact come from your best mate, or your accountant, or your grandmother. You know this because you recognise their voice, even when written rather than spoken. You know what sort of words they use, how they address you, how careful they are with their punctuation, what the quirks of their style or vocabulary are. You have a sense of their rhythms of writing e-mails, just as you'd know their patterns of speech on the phone.

When you get to know a writer's work well, you similarly begin to recognise the collection of features that distinguish their prose DNA from that of every other writer. One of the curious benefits of drafting a translation fast is that I tend to notice these things sooner. If I'm working – albeit at first *very* superficially – on maybe fifteen pages in a day, those fifteen pages are probably long enough to identify traits of this stylistic personality. I'll notice certain uncommon words if they appear more than once in a single day's work. I'll register certain little quirks of sentence structure because they're repeated in pretty quick succession.

I feel as though, now, as I work through the second half of this initial draft, I'm getting a handle on these things for Diamela's book. Those small things that she does over and over, things that would allow me, if presented – like the Pepsi challenge – with a page of this book alongside a page of some other novel by some other writer, to point to this one and confidently state, "That's it. That's her. That's definitely the, you know, the *Fire Never Something of Whatever-It's-Called* one."

Sometimes these features are tiny, but these tiny things, in composite, become the "voice" we recognise. And they're essential to be aware of if you're a translator, because those recurrences that run through the veins of the text are the fingerprints that mark them out so distinctively to a reader. (Some writers, for example, are in the habit of clumsily mixing anatomical metaphors.) If something recurs in the original, it should recur with the same sort of pulse (hooray, another one!) in the translation – which might mean needing to find consistent solutions that work across the piece and not case by case.

(I say translators need to "be aware of" these recurrences, which suggests something deliberate and conscious. They needn't be that. But they need to act upon them all the same.)

I'll give you a couple of examples of these stylistic fingerprints that I've started spotting in Diamela's book, one today and one tomorrow.

First of all, I'm going to draw your attention to her use of multiple adjectives. (Lucky old you, eh?)

The one thing you need to know about Spanish for the purposes of this is that for the most part, adjectives follow their noun:

- el hombre alto = the man tall (ie. *the tall man*, as we'd normally have it in English)
- la camisa blanca = the shirt white (ie. *the white shirt*)

and so on.

Diamela has a habit of using not just one adjective for a noun, but several.

So it might be not simply

[the house] old

but

[the house] old, big and imposing

I could, in English, just move *all* the adjectives to the front: *the big, old, imposing house.*[20]

But often, in this book, something more complicated is happening, where we're given not just a series of short unconnected adjectives but a series that delivers a sort of cumulative development. Imagine if this were the phrase instead:

I came to [a house] big, really big, actually sort of huge…

---

[20] It's annoying here that I can't follow the progression of the Spanish, because English has rules about how adjectives are sequenced – a big old house, not an old big house – and for whatever reason, my ear insists upon sticking to them.

I could flip it into the usual English order, but "I came to a big, really big, actually sort of huge house" leaves the reader hanging on for about a week not knowing what the hell the main noun is that we're talking about. (That's not always a problem, but often is.)

Or I might say something like "I came to a big house – really big, actually sort of huge", which isn't too uncomfortable to read and understand, but I think separating those "bigs" loses at least a part of that three-fold sense of progression.

What I might end up doing on such occasions is essentially maintaining Diamela's effect by keeping the Spanish word order – adjectives after nouns – which requires a little tweak to the phrasing. I can't say "he was a man tall wearing a shirt white standing outside that house funny, old". But I could say it's "a shirt that was white", perhaps. And a house that was big, really big, actually sort of huge. The shape of the sentence then follows the progressing of the thought, just like in the Spanish.

I can't do this for every adjective, of course – if I start writing "The man who was old sat on the bench that was creaky on the morning that was sunny and closed his eyes that were tired, wrinkled," this once taut book will double in length. But I suspect I'll do it a lot with at least the multiple adjectives, and especially with those that propel the sentence forward, and I'll try to maintain some stylistic consistency – this recurrence might be a bit noticeable, but I think it's noticeable when she does it, too.

Here are a few of the many I've lately encountered on my race through the book, which I'll share together with the Spanish noun-adjectives word order, the normal English adjectives-noun word order, and an alternative that might allow me to keep the effect of delaying the adjectives as the author can do naturally in Spanish:

a una reunión clandestina e impostergable
Sp: at a meeting clandestine and urgent
En: at a clandestine [and?] urgent meeting
Alt: at a meeting that is clandestine and urgent
(simple!)

los movimientos vacuos aunque previsibles que nos rigen
Sp: the movements vacuous yet predictable that
govern us
En: the vacuous but predictable movements that
govern us
Alt: the movements, vacuous but predictable, that
govern us
(I always like this solution)

un líquido frío y tenue, cristalino. Digo: cristalino
Sp: a liquid cold and fine, crystalline. I say again:
crystalline.
En: a cold, fine, crystalline liquid. I say again: crystalline.
Alt: a liquid that is cold and fine, crystalline. I say
again: crystalline.
(though not using these exact words, because the
accidental fine/crystalline rhyme is really annoying)

I have the sense – totally without hard evidence,
just occurring to me as I write – that Spanish writers
are more likely to use long strings of adjectives than
English ones (I was certainly advised not to as a student),
possibly because without any variation, an English list
gets in the way, whereas a Spanish list follows on from
the noun and therefore can be the thing that leads the
sentence onwards. As in this case from Diamela's book,
the trickiest example of all:

...se produce en mis ojos un inevitable parpadeo, veloz, esa
velocidad mecánica del cuerpo, la misma que me permite
levantarme
Sp: there is produced in my eyes an inevitable[21]
blinking, quick, that quickness mechanical of the
body, the same one that allows me to get up...

This is harder than the others because of the way
the sentence develops: it is *an inevitable blinking quick, a*
quickness mechanical – that rapid progression linking those
underlined words is much less effective in an English
version that forces them apart, saying "a quick inevitable
blinking, that mechanical quickness that..." Only by
keeping something like the Spanish word order (blinking
quick => quickness mechanical) can I keep those two
words nicely in balance the way Diamela does it. But I
can't help feeling "a blinking that is inevitable and quick,
a quickness that is mechanical" is really wordy, so it'll
need more thought. But it's worth more thought because
the novel does this *a lot*.[22]

More tomorrow, I'm afraid.

---

[21] Notice this single *pre*-noun adjective in the Spanish, to complicate
things. But whatever. I'm just ignoring it.

[22] Oh, that's not the end of the problem, incidentally. At the end of that
last quotation, you might have thought "the same one that..." referred
to "the same body", but actually it's referring to the same *quickness*
there, too – in Spanish there is no doubt because "la misma" can only
be referring to a feminine noun, so it has to be la velocidad/speed
rather than el cuerpo/body. (You may remember some of the problems
raised by moving between languages that are gendered differently, from
back on February 8.)

9 March (2)

Not a Proper Post

Just a postscript to today's earlier post. (A postpost?) Something I should have mentioned while complaining about adjectives that follow nouns...

Sometimes a list like this appears in the original:

NounA, NounB and NounC

And I will translate it as:

NounC, NounB and NounA

This seemingly wilful change is the fault of adjectives, too.

(Seriously, people, the damn things can wreak havoc.)

Imagine now that there's an adjective following the third noun:

NounA, NounB and NounC [Adjective]

Unless there's a clue in the adjective itself (if it specifies gender, number etc.), it is not always clear whether it relates to only the last of nouns – to *NounC* – or to them all.

Am I wearing a jacket, a hat and [shoes that are black]? Or am I wearing [a jacket and hat and shoes] that are black?

If I flip only the adjective and that one noun for my English translation, as in the first version – *NounA, NounB and [Adjective] NounC* – I'm deciding that I want the adjective to refer only to that last noun, unambiguously. In this case, I have no idea what colour the jacket and hat are. (I don't know why you're asking me, I'm just the translator.)

The only way of preserving this possible doubt from the original, when I'm compelled by English custom to move the adjective forward, is to move that last noun all the way up to the front of the line, too. So

Spanish: *NounA, NounB and NounC [Adjective]*

becomes

English: *[Adjective] NounC, NounB and NounA*

and the adjective could be read as connecting to the first noun or them all – ambiguous, just the way the original is.

Look at this sentence:

Yesterday, at last, schools reopened after lockdown, so there were happy parents, children and teachers all milling around the gate when I cycled past at 8 in the morning.

Does the "happy" also refer to the children and the

teachers, or only the parents in this sentence? Probably all of them – but you can't be totally sure…

This green-eggs-and-ham problem arises with surprising frequency.[23] Whenever it does, I have to choose between maintaining this possible little ambiguity (it might not be intentional on the author's part, but what if they simply intended one meaning and I guess the other?), and maintaining the author's own precise sequence of nouns, which is probably deliberate, too.

Anyway, the *real* next entry will be with you tomorrow, as promised.

---

[23] In *Green Eggs and Ham* itself, the only reason we know the ham is also green is because the book is illustrated. Diamela's book, however, is not illustrated. Which is probably for the best.

10 March

Another Idiosyncrasy, the Narrator's

I wrote yesterday about identifying those things that make a writer's voice, or a book's voice, distinctive, with one example being the way Diamela uses multiple post-noun adjectives to keep a sentence evolving. And I promised another example today, one I think is quite particular to the book – that is to say, particular not to Diamela but to this specific narrator. It's a tic of her speech, which also reflects the shifting processes of her thinking, and which I noticed happening several times in a shortish passage the other day.

Look at these two lines (and, as usual, don't worry if you don't understand the Spanish):

> *…a comprender que yo estaba atada a una naturaleza,* **la mía***, que ya había…*
> *…to understand that I was tied to a nature,* **my one***, that I had already…*
>
> *Me impresiona ese rostro,* **el tuyo***, contra la pared…*
> *I'm struck by the sight of that face,* **your one***, against the wall…*

The author – or really the *narrator* – does this a lot, giving us a noun (a nature, that face), only afterwards adding a mini-phrase asserting whose it is. Not "your face" but "that face, your one".

In different contexts, I might translate the Spanish as "that face, **your one**", or "that face, **yours**". Or I might use the word "own" – *I was tied to a nature, **my own**, which...* – yes, I rather like that.

There are also cases where we do in fact know explicitly to whom the noun belongs the first time around, but the *mine/yours* just reinforces it:

> ...*involucrados en nuestras chapas. **La mía, la tuya**.*
> ...*involved in our CHAPAS. **My one, your one**.*

Or "***Mine, yours***", or whatever.

(I haven't yet decided what to use for "chapas" in this context. But whatever they are, they're definitely *ours*.)

In some cases, I quite like the option of repeating the noun – ...*looking at that face, **your face**...* – that's quite nice, too, isn't it?

But that doesn't always work, because there are several cases where she does what I've described above *and* repeats the noun herself. Look at this:

> ...*al hospital y obtener para el niño, **el mío, mi niño**, una cama técnica, decente y eficaz...*
> ...*go to the hospital and to secure for the boy, **my one, my boy**, a bed that is technical, decent and effective...*[24]

Or

---

[24] If you've read the longer entry from March 9, you might have spotted the "that is" being deployed for this little run of adjectives.

*…un cuerpo que te obliga, **el tuyo, tu cuerpo** y su artritis…*
*…a body that is compelling you, **your one, your body** and its arthritis…*

In neither of these cases would it make sense to say "my boy" if the next (supposedly different) words are also "my boy"; or "your body" if she then goes on to say "your body" again. Just *mine/yours* might do it. In the case of the "niño", I'm contemplating going with the idea of "my own", which feels very affectionate – "el mío" refers to this "niño" often.

The boy. My own. My boy.

Finding a solution that works case by case is actually quite easy. But because it's one of those things that recurs, I would ideally like to treat the phenomenon the same way each time, so it marks the narrator's English voice just as it does her Spanish one – after all, I'd like a reader of the translated Diamela to be able to recognise a bit of her writing just as confidently as a reader of her original might.

At a quick search through the pdf of the original, some version of this formulation occurs more than fifty times in this short book. I might at some point ask Diamela about what she's intending by this sort of thing in the novel, her one. For now, though, my first draft is just about marking these as I go, so I'll make a point of returning to them at some stage and trying to resolve all the instances together. Having only noticed this patterning some way into the draft, I'll also have to scan through the earlier parts of the book to make sure I catch any I might have missed there, too. And that's par for the course – the whole translation process never feels straight-linear to me, but iterative.

Can't believe I'm still on iteration 1, though.

Still, on we go…

11 March

Slightly More than I'd Bargained for...

I fear I might have written recently that I'd hoped to be finished with the first draft by tomorrow.

As of this moment, my current projection is that I'll be done with it by a week today instead.

And yet I am – you will be surprised to learn – absolutely back up to speed (thankfully) and on target for productivity this week. So why the apparent delay?

Well, you know how I mentioned back on February 21 that this novel is very short, coming in at about 30,000 words? Turns out, it's about 45,000 words. Which is, you know, *several* words more.

I'm as surprised as anyone. Though in hindsight, that explains a lot, now I think about it.

Still, there we are: 45,000 it is! But as a result, I will need some of next week to make up that extra 15k.

So anyway...

12 March

And Still More Adjectives…

On the question of how adjectives might be over-used in Spanish (which I was grumbling about on Tuesday), Dan S. has submitted a comment in which he reports having been advised against this in Spanish writing schools – choose the right noun carefully and you won't need that string of adjectives. Likewise I do remember being told at university that when a writer uses two adjectives it's often because they haven't got quite the *right* adjective. And obviously that's not always the case and there can be very good reasons for using more than one, but having had that pointed out to me, it's surprising how often I find it to be the case. (In my own writing, certainly.) I think it works a little differently in Spanish anyway (not least because they follow rather than precede, so the effect in a sentence isn't the same – a list of adjectives doesn't make you wait longer for the noun as it does in English); and Diamela is certainly not doing it as a matter of carelessness – part of what makes the effect interesting in her work is how often they are part of an evolving thought, a feature that doesn't slow the sentence down but rather keeps it moving.

If you happen to be a Spanish-speaker, take a look at the word "primitivas" here, for instance, and how it carries the sentence forward:

...porque las palabras estaban allí para recubrir su muerte, para acompañarla y quizás precipitarla con palabras inútiles, palabras mortajas, elementales, primitivas ante la impotencia de la asfixia que ocurría a centímetros de unas caras que desde ese momento se iban a vaciar, las nuestras, esas que cargaríamos y que nos acusarían por el acto incomprensible de sobrevivir.

(A prime candidate for adding a "that are" or two, I reckon.)

And another good comment from Vineet yesterday, about that problem with the single adjectives and multiple nouns:

This is a really interesting one and I'm sure I've had to deal with it (probably less consciously) many times over. I was reflecting on French in particular, though, and your example of the jacket, hat and shoes being black (or not). In French you'd have a "noirs" at the end, and you wouldn't know whether it was just the shoes or indeed all 3 items of clothing. However, if it was "hat, shoes and jacket" (different order in French) and you still had "noirs" with an S, you would know (definitively) it was all 3 (I think – unless it was just 2 of the 3? Even grammar books refuse to deal with that permutation!). And if it was JUST the jacket you'd have "noir" (no S) and, again, you'd know it was definitively only the jacket. In essence, I guess, and certainly with French, there will probably be quite a few clues to help you narrow down the possibilities, and in my experience true ambiguity (as in your example) isn't as common as cases where, with a bit of grammar detective work, I can "attach" the adjective to the relevant noun (or nouns). It does feel like being in the dissection room!

Yes, that example I used is helpfully neat because there's one plural noun only, so the effect would be different if it was sequenced differently. (If the final noun was singular, then there would never be ambiguity, because the adjective either would be plural or it wouldn't.) The more usual case is having lots of plurals – as in my second example, where there are parents, teachers, childrenses, etc., and you'll never know if the adjective is just referring to the one plural or to the plural plurals, as it were.

It's also true that it wouldn't be hard for a writer to avoid ambiguity if they wanted to – just as in English there would have been ways of phrasing that parents/ teachers/children sentence so it was unquestionably clear what the adjective referred to – but the writer has to be aware that the potential misunderstanding is there if they are to act upon it, and I suspect they often just assume it means what they think it means and don't even register the alternative reading. It's only when the text gets read – by a translator, by an editor, by any other reader – that all the possible misreadings against which they failed to legislate are suddenly unleashed.

14 March

Guys and Dolls

I mentioned the other day that my translation process feels not linear but iterative, and one of the functions of the first draft is identifying those things I need to figure out in my second pass, my third, and however many might follow thereafter.

Sometimes the uncertainties are obvious at first sight – I know up-front that they're unknowns, if you like – as is the case with some of the examples I've cited already. (Do I, as I wondered on 12 February, include a "the" before a noun?) There are familiar words that can have more than one common meaning, and so long as both are plausible in the context, I'll typically keep both options at this stage and mark it for later consideration. When I return to this part of the book, these sorts of things will usually be obvious right away.

I know, for instance, that whenever I see a first reference to a character's *hijos* – as on page 19 of this novel – I <u>always</u> have to check whether this is referring to their *children* or their *sons*. *Abuelos* might be *grandparents*, but occasionally could just be *grandfathers*, too. Collectives in

Spanish default to the masculine, as I explained a few weeks ago, so I need to be alert not to close off multiple possibilities whatever my first translation instinct might be. (I recently translated a piece in which the narrator discusses and challenges this very issue of the masculine default at some length himself, creating a whole other layer of translation trouble. I used the helpful English word "guys" quite a lot to get around it.)[25]

Occasionally, though, I can breeze past a problem quite obliviously, and it's only later in the text – which might be the next paragraph or a hundred pages on – that I realise there was anything tricky happening at all.

Never Did the Fire is narrated by a woman, who is in a room with a man. Both central characters are unnamed. (At least, so far. They might yet be named in the remaining few dozen pages, but I'd be surprised.) There's a bed, a table, a chair; there's a kitchen next door, and a bathroom down the hall. A lot of the novel takes place in this one room, or happens elsewhere as remembered from this room. The narrator goes out only occasionally, the man is mostly bedbound and hardly leaves at all. She recalls their days as militants in various political cells, alongside her descriptions of the present. The book is also about the increasing dilapidation of their bodies, so that other kind of *cell* is significant, too. At one point, the man, whose multiple pains and ailments take up a lot of the narrator's attention, tells her that his wrist is aching: "Me duele la muñeca". It's a perfectly normal sentence. I mean, I suppose you *could* find an ambiguity in it because *muñeca* (wrist) also means *doll* but you'd have to be trying pretty hard – he has pains in his hand, knee, back, teeth, etc. and now, apparently, his wrist. The "doll" ambiguity here is only theoretical and irrelevant – no Spanish reader would

[25] The piece in question was David Aliaga's "Insomnia of the Statues", from Granta's *Best of Young Spanish-Language Novelists 2*.

be distracted by it, I suspect, so I can disregard it and keep moving.

But something odd happens now. The narrator gives the man a hard time – she repeats the word *wrist* half a dozen times in the paragraph: Oh, your wrist hurts, does it? Which wrist? Where exactly does your wrist hurt? etc. It's surprising, and feels quite out of the blue. But why does she do it? Because, as it soon transpires, she believes that he's using the word intentionally to bother her, because of that really destabilising incident, all those years ago, when some guy in a meeting patronisingly called her a *muñeca* – a doll – which she still remembers very bitterly.

The first time the word flitted past, I translated it simply enough – ...*my wrist hurts*... – and didn't bother marking it as needing further thought, because, well, why would I? Plenty of other more likely problems to stress about. But it soon became clear that there was more going on than I'd realised, and that I will in fact have to return to this later and find a good solution. I'll also have to check that the word hasn't appeared <u>earlier</u> in the book, as I might have to tinker with those other occurrences, too. What we readers learn on page 84 will inform our reading of everything that comes afterwards – but for the reading experience to be complete, it's got to inform my translation of pages 1-83 just as much.

(A few possible ways around this particular problem have already come to mind, and I can share them if you're interested, though currently I like none of them. I guess I could always have the man initially saying "My wrist hurts, doll", but then I'd have to transpose the entire novel, *lock, stock y barril* to the U.S. in the 1920s, and that might be going a bit far.)

I should say one last thing, in general terms, about ambiguity, because this book is full of it. (The back-cover blurb of the Spanish edition makes great play of this fact.) I mentioned very early in this diary that ambiguity can be the hardest thing to translate. I think some people imagine ambiguity as a kind of vagueness, but to my mind you might better consider it exactly the opposite, as an extreme sort of precision, and that's what makes it hard. When it's meaningful and deliberate, it doesn't open up your options, it narrows them. The word or phrase you're after doesn't only have to mean x, it has to mean x *and also* y. The Spanish word *historia* means both *history* and *story*, whereas English splits those meanings over two common words – in an ideal world, I'd find one English word that did precisely both; in practice, I probably have to choose for each occurrence which one I'm going to plump for. (This is a book about telling stories about history, so the choice won't always be as obvious as it might seem.) I'm lucky that English uses the word "cells" for units of a militant group as well as for the building blocks of an organism, just as Spanish uses *células*, but more often than not, the ambiguity in the original has no equivalent in my translation language.

Oh, and turns out – complicating things further – the characters in this book even have a conversation *about* ambiguity. Who the hell thought translating this was a good idea?

On the plus side, by the next time you hear from me (Thursday, I reckon), I should be able to report having finished this somewhat-longer-than-expected first draft. Then I'll have only the really difficult parts of the process left. Can't wait.

15 March

Hmm, I've just come across the opposite problem to the gender-specifying one described on 8 February. In today's text, a chapter begins with a character saying "[X] isn't eating", followed by a conversation about why the person in question isn't eating – where [X] in my English sentence is standing in for the pronoun. The conversation at this point could in theory refer to a number of different characters, male or female, but Spanish can be ambiguous because it can dispense with pronouns in sentences like these altogether. It becomes clear further down the page that it's one of the female characters who's being discussed, so I probably have to open the chapter with "She", but that means the reader's provisional doubt in the original won't be there in the translation. Not sure how to get around it yet.

16 March

Where I Went Wrong

With reference to last week's entry, Sue has written to ask how the word count came to be so wildly wrong. This does not seem an unreasonable question. And the answer is, well, there's no mysterious reason, just usual human folly. (Mostly mine, in this case, as so often.) I was guided in my planning by the estimate we put in the contract I signed with the publishers; what I'd forgotten (since the contract was signed a really long time ago) was that neither the publisher nor I actually knew the word count of the book at the moment when we signed – we hadn't even had sight of the pdf at that point – but we knew it was very short (148 printed pages in the Spanish), so just put some quite small number there as a placeholder. And then when we got hold of the pdf of the book, we never went back to it.

Because the fee is defined "per word", and thus flexes with the word count, it doesn't necessarily matter in practical terms what word count the contract cites – unless the translator foolishly uses it to plan his schedule. And when I was some way into the book, I had a glance at the contract to help to calibrate my progress a bit in order to describe it in this diary, and forgot just how vague that estimate had been! (Certainly helps to explain why

I felt like I was progressing really slowly…) The problem only became clear when I was approaching the 30k mark in my translation and seemed to have a strangely large numbers of pages left, at which point I checked the pdf and discovered why this was. Not a mistake I intend to repeat.

18 March

End of Part One

I often use a pdf of the original text to translate from, and I'll have a working version of that file on my desktop and delete the pages as I go – the working pdf, then, is not of the whole original book but of however much of the original book remains to be translated. (I have a friend who numbers the book's pages in reverse order, which has a similar effect: you're always aware not only of how far you've gone – the regular page numbers – but how far is left to go.) Deleting the pages I've just translated at the end of a session is satisfying. Even more satisfying is that point when you're finally approaching the end of the book and you can look at the scroll bar and see the thumb increase proportionately as the number of outstanding pages dwindles. Small pleasures.

Anyway, today I reached the last page of the original, the scroll bar disappeared, and shortly afterwards I had arrived at the last line – ...*because, after all, we have nothing left to lose.* – and the pages-left-to-do pdf could be dragged and dropped into the trash.

My first draft is done. It took me rather longer than planned (for a range of reasons I shared on February 14, March 3 and March 11), but we're there at last. Very pleased to have made it, in some form, to the final line.

(Also: what a *great* book, by the way.)

The word count of my current Word doc – "Diamela EN live draft" – stands at 48,954, but that tally includes countless little queries and notes to myself, multiple options for some words etc., so by the time I've removed those extraneous things and tightened up the whole lot, the final count should be rather shorter. (I don't have the Spanish book as a Word doc so I don't know how many words make up the original novel, but in my experience, my translations tend to come out very slightly longer than their sources.)

I'll be spending the next few days basically looking things up. Multiple dictionaries, Wikipedia, and whatever else I might need. I'll let you know how it goes.

19 March

Ooh, given that I get paid by the word, I wonder if I should invoice the publishers *now*, at the point at which the book is at its absolute longest? Normally I'd draw up my invoice with the delivered manuscript, but this does seem like a missed opportunity – so many unnecessary words I could be billing for! I mean, there are only so many extra adjectives I can scatter about at the last minute to bump the numbers up.

(Don't tell them I do this, obviously.)

21 March

Things are Looking Up!

Having got through the initial slog, and put that first draft down on paper – it's all in a shocking state, obviously, but at least it's no longer just 178 blank pages – I've spent much of the last 48 hours looking words up in the dictionary.

My first pass at the text left several thousand of the most troublesome words in Spanish, and because Charco probably won't want to publish the book if I've just ignored all the difficult bits (publishers always make such unreasonable demands…), this next stage is unavoidable. Fortunately, in many cases, checking a word in the dictionary or some other reference source and dropping the answer into the English text is a simple enough matter. These simple lookings-up at this stage fall into a few general categories:

1. Spanish words I just don't know at all. Of course, there are loads of words I sort of half-know, and/or words I can half-intuit from context, and fortunately there aren't a *lot* of words that

are totally, entirely mysterious to me, but even those do show up occasionally. The Spanish words for *retching*, *tarnish*, *cramp*, and a few others are completely new to my vocabulary as of this weekend. I looked up the respective Spanish words, and duly slotted these English words into the text. I almost certainly won't remember these bits of Spanish vocab by this time next week, incidentally. (The only words I do actually seem to learn are the ones that recur many times in a text. I know that the Portuguese word *bisturi* means *scalpel*, and also which book I picked it up from, because it cropped up there over and over again, and even I am bound to learn something eventually.)

2. Words the author uses that I <u>think</u> I know, but want to be sure. I don't remember having used *escrutinio*, *exasperarse* or *deviacionismo* before, and while I'd guess they probably mean *scrutiny*, *to become exasperated* and *deviationism*, I'll always check this kind of thing. Too tempting to assume and be wrong. (Note to self: because it appears several times, at some point I really must learn what *deviationism* means <u>in English</u>.) I'm pretty sure *zapatillas* can be used to refer to slippers as well as other common types of footwear, but I wanted to check this, too. Oh, and medical references to *calcificaciones* are surely *calcifications*, but it can't hurt to look it up. (Though in fact my draft has the words *calificaciones* rather than *calcificaciones*. One of the things my first draft teaches me is how sloppy my typing is when I can't depend on autocorrect. I presume my *norotia* is meant to be *notoria*, and so on and on

112

and on. These things send me back repeatedly to the original at this stage just to check that this peculiar word copied into my draft, pretending to be Spanish, really is just a typo for something much more obvious.)

3. <u>English</u> words I'm not sure about. The draft is also littered with notes to myself saying *[En?]* or similar. My problem in these cases is either a doubt about English usage, or a prompt to hunt down a word that for some reason just didn't come immediately to mind when I was drafting. I know that the word *impostergable* is an adjective meaning *unable-to-be-postponed*; but I have no idea whether *unpostponable* is a word or whether I just made it up. The draft says "unpostponable *[En?]*" and I'm checking that this weekend, too. Likewise *unconcealable*, and a use of *hang* as a noun to refer to the appearance of a piece of clothing, and many more. (I think *equanimity* can mean what I want it to mean in this context, but that's one to check, too.) Sometimes these are phrases where even in the drafting process, even without thinking about it, I knew already that there was something wrong and that a bit of gentle rephrasing would be called for. (Would we say "The feeling that opens up a path *[En?]* in my mind is…"? We would not.)

4. The other part of this looking-up stage is the non-linguistic research, checking actual information rather than dictionary meanings or language use. In the case of this book, that includes checking eight quotations that the narrator drops into discussion at various points. The first

to appear is "The workers have no homeland. It is not possible to take away from them what they do not possess." It's not hard to guess that this is from *The Communist Manifesto*. As it turns out, that's where all eight quotations come from. Their appearances in the novel aren't all quite accurate as per the *Manifesto* itself, which I suspect is intentional, but I'll have to confirm that, too.

Even after two days, I'm nowhere near done with this looking-up process. I'd guess I'm about half-way? Though the truth is, I don't know exactly what proportion I've done, because I don't start at the beginning and work through in sequence, but jump around. This isn't just for morale, though, it's also practical, because so many words recur multiply in a text – once I've found out what one of these troublesome words/phrases means, I'll search through and often end up plugging it into several places over the course of the book; then I'll just find the next problem to solve wherever I've happened to end up.

But while there's a lot still to do, this part of the process is strangely satisfying. A bit boring, but satisfying. Plugging the gaps makes what looked like sheer linguistic carnage begin to resemble a piece of continuous text. A piece of continuous text that still requires huge amounts of editorial work, of course, but substantially more like a finished thing. Look at these two paragraphs – you don't even need to read the words, just glance at their appearance. What was previously

I pass unnoticed, my studied* insignificance, that can save us, oh no, no, never save us, not even RESGUARDO us my deep OPACIDAD [opacity/opaqueness – En?]. The light comes in DE MANERA CAUTA, a light that is altogether* OBTURADA. The time is

approaching. Yes, remember that I told you. We should make a decision. I was crying because I was ATER-RORIZADA, I knew what was going to happen. We must hurry, take him to the hospital. Either you take him or I will. No, no, no, it's impossible, impossible. Soon I'm going to go out and it's cloudy [nublado – overcast?], with that grey that ACHATA the landscape, LO PONE EN a level of INCOMODO realism, a landscape that isn't worth it. Doesn't mean anything. The grey.

is now, somewhat less stressfully,

I pass unnoticed, my studied insignificance, that can save us, oh no, no, never save us, not even my deep opacity shielded us. The light comes in cautiously, a light that is altogether★ blocked. The time is approaching. Yes, remember I told you. We should make a decision. I was crying because I was terrified, I knew what was going to happen. We must hurry, take him to the hospital. Either you take him or I will. No, no, no, it's impossible, impossible. Soon I'm going to go out and it's overcast, with that grey that flattens the landscape, LO PONE EN a level of uncomfortable/tiresome realism, a landscape that isn't worth it. Doesn't mean anything. The grey.

This is still very far from being anything I'd be happy to share with readers (remind me why I'm giving you access to this diary again?), but you can see it does at least look like, well, *something*. (The word count of the first draft, as described on March 18, was 48,954, and it's already lost about 400 words just from tidying up some of the mess.)

As I said above, very many cases in this looking-up stage are simple enough. Find out what a word means, or check an English usage, or a quote, and just plug the gap.

But – and isn't there always one of those? – the others are not as straightforward. I'll be inflicting those more problematic ones on you tomorrow.

(I'll also try to remember to say a little about which reference sources I'm using, because, well, there's no telling what weird things people will find interesting…)

22 March

Minding the Gaps

If you've read yesterday's entry, you'll know that I'm currently spending a few days plugging gaps in the draft. I gave some examples of the sorts of things I was doing – looking up words I didn't know in the dictionary, stuff like that. Nothing massively strenuous, it must be said. But today's problems are trickier. Because often the challenge is not figuring out what the original means, it's figuring out how to replicate whatever it's doing in this new language. I'll share some examples of these pending problems today. Here's one:

My draft still has the words *comprender, pared, década, esperar* and *cara* in Spanish. Why? After all, they're pretty common words: *understand, wall, decade, wait* and *face*. Nice and easy.

Other words currently still in Spanish include *entender, muro, decenio, aguardar* and *rostro*. These mean… *understand, wall, decade, wait* and *face*.

I need to figure out how to differentiate between understanding and understanding, walls and walls, decades and decades, waiting and waiting, and faces and faces. Sometimes it's easy (sometimes, for example, a character's *face* is really their *expression*), usually it is not. The problem, however, is entirely the English, I have no trouble understanding the Spanish. Nor, for that matter, understanding it.

It would matter less if it weren't for the fact that these pairs of words – defaulting to the same English translation – often appear in quick succession. (I believe that this is because the author apparently hates me. I can't think of any other reason at this point.) So I need to find a workaround to avoid adding a repetition that isn't there in the original. Lines currently in my draft include:

> *"I do understand [comprendo], I understand [entiendo] your need to…"*
> *"I watch your migraine-stricken, dark face [cara], the years on our faces [rostros]…"*
> *"She sits there with her head tilted, waiting [esperando]. She waits [aguarda] while I…"*

(You'll remember the pair of non-identical *nevers* that bedevilled the title, too, of course.)

Spanish also usually differentiates between internal corners (the corner in a room, say), and external corners (like the corner of a street). The former is *rincón*, the latter *esquina*. Except for the moment on page 108 where the narrator refers to something happening in the *esquina* of the room. In other words, perhaps, <u>on</u> *the corner of the room* rather than <u>in</u> *the corner of the room*? Or…? No, me neither.[26]

Where words split the other way – i.e., one Spanish word with at least two markedly different English meanings – that creates trouble, too, of course. How do I know which

---

[26] A later note-with-hindsight from the translator: as this diary goes to press, I have just found another of my writers - Guatemalan, in this case - repeatedly using "esquina" for the inside of a room. Always learning new things! (Albeit, in this case, rather belatedly.)

eficaz is *efficient* and which is *effective*? Context sometimes helps, but not always.

(At least context can usually tell me whether a character *sits down on a bed* or *sits up in bed*. The Spanish reveals nothing, so I need to know what position they were <u>previously</u> in if I'm to deduce what this action is. Likewise when the narrator is *sitting on a chair* and when she's *sitting in a chair* – Spanish uses the same prepositions for both, while in English I'd differentiate based on, among other things, what sort of chair I imagine it is. The more spacious and comfortable and enveloping and armchairy the piece of furniture is, the more *in* it the sitter will be, I think.)

Then there are other words whose meaning I do know, but that are just very hard to convey economically in English – so these remain pending problems. I don't need to look them up, I just need a brainwave that at this point I'm not sure will ever happen. Spanish has the word *auscultar* for the verb *to sound*, specifically in the sense of a doctor sounding a patient's chest; I know we have the word *auscultate* in English, but it's preposterous in comparison – how commonly do we English-speakers really use that word figuratively? A *bulto* is a shape, but a three-dimensional one, a sort of lump, some solid object, a bulky, voluminous thing – and perhaps my most hated word of all to translate. In this book, the wretched thing appears four times in the space of one page.

And then there are the words whose meaning I know, and which can be easily conveyed in English, but whose <u>register</u> is quite hard to replicate. There are two brief scenes with a few references to faeces, using the word *caca*, which is neither medical nor especially vulgar, and nothing in English quite works. And talking about faeces, North American readers of this diary would spell the word without an "a", and that's a whole other problem: this translation is going to be published simultaneously across the Anglosphere, and there are several places in the text where it's very hard to avoid what feels like locally specific English. (Currently my rendering of the scene in question uses *diapers* rather than *nappies*. Yet the narrator arrives at this same scene via a *pavement* rather than a *sidewalk*.) The mirror of this problem is that the original book has words whose use is only Latin American, or even particular to the continent's Southern Cone, or even more specifically Chilean. I'll write about these – the challenges of reconciling multiple Spanishes and multiple Englishes – in a later entry.

There are many words that recur an unusual number of times, most of which likewise remain in Spanish as still unsolved problems. Again, it's not that I don't know their meaning, but I don't know which word to choose for them if I'm going to keep the consistency. These three get used figuratively: *invadido* (23 times), *desencadenar* (14 times), *entregado* (42 times). Two characters wear a *delantal* (which spans an apron, an overall and other things) but I'd call their respective pieces of clothing by two different names in English – is it OK to lose the connection? Hmm, these recurrences probably deserve their own entry at some point, too.

And finally (for now), there are those words whose meanings I know, but which I left in the Spanish because I noticed something else going on that I wasn't going to solve in that draft but wanted to keep in mind. That wrist/ doll trouble, say. Or the scene, for instance, in which the characters are talking about reading the newspaper, and the man doesn't want to keep reading because of his headache. Their reading, figuring out the world by assembling stories into a big composite picture, is compared to a *rompecabezas* – which is a jigsaw puzzle. But literally the Spanish word means something like "head-breaker", so it's very explicitly pre-empting the headache two lines down. Short of reframing it as a "head-scratcher" or a "brainteaser" or another common English term, my translation has lost the connection. Again, the problem isn't that I don't know what the Spanish is doing, it's that as yet I haven't figured out a way of replicating it in English, so for now, the Spanish word remains stubbornly untranslated.

(One possible solution to this one, incidentally, would be to do something with the word *headlines* in the same paragraph – the Spanish word *titulares* doesn't contain the word *head* like the English does, so that might be an almost-adequate compensation?)

So – all yet to be resolved. And of course, as I said in the last entry, there's also all that stuff I simply <u>don't know</u>, where my Spanish itself is inadequate. This happens more often than I'd like. The truth is, I'm always relieved when I look up a Spanish word – or ask a Hispanophone friend – and it turns out to be reasonably obscure. So *Noto que la piel de su espalda está engranujada* means *I notice that the skin on her back is…* what? Sometimes neither I nor (reassuringly) my dictionaries have any idea what's going on.

I have so far been using online dictionaries – Reverso for a quick check of the low-hanging fruit, and WordReference. Some things that elude those sources might send me to the big old hardback Collins dictionary on the shelf (I'll do this tomorrow). I've also ordered a little book of Chilean-specific vocabulary, which should be arriving in the post sometime this week. And for other non-linguistic things, I've spent a lot of time on Wikipedia and, of course, rummaging around in *The Communist Manifesto*.

Over the coming days, the five million still outstanding queries will gradually narrow to those that seem most intractable, where the sources readily at my disposal can't help me, at which point I will start asking Hispanophone friends and family. Later, when things get more desperate still, that's when I'll be putting my leftover questions to the author. But we're nowhere near that point yet.

26 March

Status Report

Just a brief status report today:

By the end of Sunday, I should be done plugging most of my gaps in this draft. I'm sure there will still be *some* left, but maybe a couple per page rather than a dozen. Those remaining will either be things that are especially challenging, or things I just couldn't quite face mustering the effort to solve at the moment I looked at them (for reasons of temporary motivation rather than actual linguistic difficulty) and to which I simply need to return at some point when feeling more inspired.

Having told you a few days ago that the word count had dropped by about 400 words, it's now back up again, not because I'm regressing (I hope), but because quite a lot of the moments on which I've been working are now retaining two or more options/choices/alternatives/possibilities. (A quick search tells me I've got about 350 slashes in the manuscript, and that number is likely to go up before it comes down.)

Many of those binary choices

unforeseen/unexpected?
force/strength?
were detached/came away?
managed/governed/run?
punctilious/picky?
etc.
(/ and so on)

will be resolved next week when I read the translation through in full for the first time, because my selection in each case will be based mostly on the specific context (how the word fits into the narrator's train of thought, the rhythm of her sentences and things like that), and once you've got the momentum of a sentence, it's often immediately apparent which is the optimal choice of word to fill a gap. (In some ways, that's the hardest part of the process to describe, because of its you–just–know–it–when–you–see–it quality that makes one word obviously what I need and the other obviously not.)

In the meantime, I have a few more hours of looking things up and pondering options. My little Chilean-specific "dictionary and phrasebook" arrived yesterday, so I'll be checking some usages in there, too. The "phrasebook" part of it is arranged thematically, and there's a section entitled "Sloth and Indifference", so I like it already.[27] I'll also have twenty minutes in the car with my Chilean stepdad tomorrow, so he may get some questions.

Just one other place I might consult as a penultimate resort (the author being the last) is the Brazilian edition

---

[27] If you're curious about this, and need several pages of Chilean "sloth and indifference" slang in your life, the phrasebook in question is *Chilenismos*, by Daniel Joelson.

of this novel. The Brazilian translation of Diamela's book was done by the brilliant Julián Fuks (who happens conveniently to be my other Charco author[28]), and there are quite a few moments where I'm curious to know what he's done for his version. Portuguese translations of Spanish books don't always help enormously with problem-solving, as those languages are close enough that, for example, many of the ambiguities are common to both and so a Portuguese translator doesn't need to make choices as I do for English; but there are at least a handful of moments where I'd like to see how Julián read a particular sentence and if he went the same way as me. ("Either of these things could be the subject of the verb, and I'm inclined to think it's this one – that's not crazy, right?") I won't necessarily be able to use any of his solutions, nor might I be inclined to, but using the translation essentially as a way of getting the insights of another close reader of the novel can't hurt.

Next week the reading and editing begins, so I'll share some living text with you then.

P.S. In recent happy news, I've managed this week to use the words "entreaty", "equivocate", "listlessness", "furtive", "flail" and "meticulous", and they are all words I like a lot. Always grateful for any excuse to deploy the good ones.

---

[28] I think we're going to be using Julián's introduction for our edition, too. Must get around to translating that at some point.

30 March

Habemus Something Resembling a Draft

Hallelujah.

This feels like progress. I've looked up most of the things I needed to look up, and I've made a few small choices. There's still a lot missing (and many, many edits ahead), but at least the manuscript now actually looks like the draft of a novel and no longer like an explosion in a multilingual nonsense factory. So, well, that's something.

A few of the things I've been reminded of in the last few days:

- If I'm honest, sometimes when choosing between a couple of options for a word, one of the criteria that plays a part is simply which word I like the most. Today I had one of those rare cases where I was struggling because basically I really like both alternatives: so is the narrator's approach going to be *furtive* or *stealthy*? This language spoils me sometimes. I also like the word "baleful" enough that I found myself trying quite hard to crowbar it into a sentence where it probably doesn't belong. (Great, though, isn't it?)

- *Bread* is, for a seemingly simple noun, surprisingly hard to translate.
- English does great verbs: I just took a phrase which in Spanish was something like "I pulled up with great and abrupt strength" and translated it as "I yanked". Other words continue frustratingly to non-exist, however. I need an adjective to describe a person who is waiting for something (which isn't "waiting"), which doesn't give any indication as to whether they think the thing they await will be good (*expectant!*) or bad (*apprehensive!*). If you have any suggestions, I'll be here sitting waitingly.
- Prepositions are really annoying.
- We usually rely on context to tell us which of two or more possible meanings is the most likely. So while I learned this week, for example, that the word "palo" not only means "stick" but is also used specifically in Chile to refer to a million pesos, nonetheless, going on probability, the scene in which a character is badly beaten with a *palo* almost certainly intends the first meaning – she isn't, I'm pretty confident, being viciously assaulted with large wads of banknotes. (That said, I was surprised to find more than one sentence that could work equally well with the word "camera" or "chamber" in them; likewise "room" and "piece".)

A few new things I've learned:

- That point I just made about being able to deduce meanings from context doesn't always work if you have a writer who actively enjoys using words in unlikely ways. This is, and will continue to be, a problem. There are even two instances of words in this book which, if it were any other writer, I'd think they were typos for very similar but much more obvious words, but here, maddeningly, I just can't be sure. More on this to come, I suspect.

- *Alero* is the Spanish for *eaves*. Another lovely new word to forget before the week is up.

- Car accidents seem to be dealt with differently in Chile, in legal terms. It's got something to do with judges. Haven't grasped this entirely yet – still pending further investigation.

- The Brazilian translation of this book, which I mentioned a few days ago, includes two translator's footnotes – one of them to explain what a *frentista* is (as per my February 1 entry), and one to gloss the *wrist/doll* wordplay (my entry on March 14). I have unreasonably strong feelings about using footnotes, but wonder whether this is a book in which I should maybe just get over myself. I used a couple of them in my very first book translation a thousand years ago, and have managed to avoid them since; but I could, I suppose, make an exception?[29]

- There are several more or less sing-able English translations of "The Internationale" and I don't really love any of them.

Tomorrow I start reading. Having put all the various slippery bits back into the novel and sewn it all up again,

---

[29] I'm slightly compromised, though: I once casually remarked to an author that I considered a footnote in a translated novel to be an admission of defeat – that author then quoted me saying exactly this in one of his books, and the book in question appears in English this summer. Never say things to authors.

now is the stage when I find out if the patient still has a pulse. I'll let you know.

4 April

Assorted Suggestions

Lots of useful comments have been coming in, responding to recent entries. Several people have written with suggestions for neutral *waiting* words. Paul suggested doing something with "linger", and Tereze offered "in anticipation", which might also work. I liked Mara's "on tenterhooks", which to me certainly sounds more eager (eagerer? eagrier?) than just sort of neutrally waiting, but that might be OK. In all of these cases, though, it'll depend on how much the sentence will require reframing, since none of these are regular single-word adjectives, and one of those would be ideal. But I'll see what I can do – they're all on the list for now.

And a few people offered suggestions for "engranujada", most of them seeming to think it's referring to something like goosebumps (Dan tracked down a Dominican website I'd not found, which seems to support this). That was certainly the meaning I guessed from the context (the line after observing the woman's skin is the narrator asking "Are you cold?") and a possible etymology that Dan refers to is a clue, but I hadn't yet found any confirmation anywhere. Turns out, on googling, that *engranujada/o* is an obscure word that Diamela herself has used in other books. (Remember how I wrote on March 9th that each writer has a particular DNA to their language use? This might be a very tiny example of that.) My pending decision here, having more or less resolved the meaning (with, I'd say, 95% certainty), is whether simply to use "goosebumps", or to try for better equivalence by finding something less obvious in English, given that this is hardly the most generically used Spanish word. Worth some thought…

Radhika and Aron wrote about assorted *puzzles/ rompecabezas*. And on the subject of footnotes, Ann shared the story of a Swedish translator attempting to use one to explain what a ceilidh is, despite clearly being somewhat hazy on the matter himself.

(OK, that last one wasn't *useful* exactly, but I liked it.)

5 April

First Read I (General Entry)

By the end of today, I'll have completed my first full read-through of the draft translation. Verdict? It is <u>not terrible</u>. It's a million miles from good, but good wasn't what I was expecting at this point, so even not-terrible feels like a win.

I've been reading on paper, and scribbling notes on it as I go along, so the next stage is for me to incorporate all those notes into the Word doc, and print it out again, and read it again, and scribble on it again. Rinse and repeat. (I don't always do this stage on paper, though I much prefer it. I am doing so in this case, because it's a particularly tricky text that'll need a lot of fiddly work, and because it's short enough that even three full printings won't be a massive environmental calamity.)

So what have I found in my first full draft, and – in general terms – what have I been doing to it?

Well, the easy thing first: I've been correcting mistakes. When the narrator says "it was almost as it we were engaged in a kind of protracted dance", the second *it* is clearly supposed to be an *if*. It's not a stylistic oddity, just a symptom of my sloppiness when typing fast. "The meaning went on for eight hours", you say? No, it was definitely a *meeting*.

Then there are those things I stumbled across that, well, *might* be mistakes, but I'm not 100% sure. One of the commonest marks on my draft pages is [chk], which will send me back to double-check (dbl-chk?) the word or phrase against the original. Most pages have at least one of these. There's a sudden tense change in the paragraph, but is that really supposed to be there? It wasn't just a little first-draft slip on my part? That repetition of "ourselves" in two consecutive sentences, we're sure that's intentional, right? These moments are always instructive, because even if I confirm that I haven't made a mistake as such, the fact that it felt wrong as I read it still tells me I need to do <u>something</u> to it – yeah, this change of tense is clearly deliberate, OK, but obviously it needs to be managed less jarringly in my translation somehow because it sure as hell doesn't work yet.

As there are still a few hundred little doubts left over from the previous version – places where I've left myself more than one option, or where I wasn't sure quite what the author was intending – I'll resolve some of these in this first read, too. Sometimes the meaning of a previously obscure sentence will become suddenly clear when read through smoothly in the context of its whole paragraph. Sometimes the selection of word *A* rather than its synonym *B* will become instantly obvious and easy. (Or sometimes an entirely new option will suggest itself. The always-problematic Spanish word "destino" means both "destiny" and "destination", and it's not always apparent which meaning should predominate when I need to choose, but during this read, I did toy with replacing an equivocating "destiny/destination" with a definite "purpose", which does exactly what I need it to do.)

This draft will still have a lot of doubts outstanding when I'm done with it, but, well, fewer. Progress is slow and iterative, but progress all the same.

However, most of the things I've been changing in this draft are not the correction of mistakes, or the resolution of problems. So what are they? They're the things that start to make bad writing into good writing, I suppose. Small things mostly, sometimes no greater than a syllable or a comma, but whose cumulative effect is that the reader will experience their journey through this prose as I wish them to. Sometimes this involves tending to a slightly tangled phrase that can easily be untangled; sometimes it's a moment where just a simple comma would make the sense of the sentence much easier to follow with no great loss of effect. I'll typically remove a lot of surplus words at this stage (the word "that" will disappear several dozens of times, where it was a non-negotiable part of the original's sentence architecture but we don't need it in English: "he told me that he was going to the cinema" etc.). And I'll make quite a lot of decisions about contractions. A lot of cases of "I am" will become "I'm" – and also vice versa – whenever it's necessary to make the voice seem more normal to my ear.

But wait: there is a danger inherent in this stage of the process. Sure, I do often want to contract verbs (*don't, can't*), because that's natural to me whenever I write or speak myself – almost every sentence in my last paragraph has such a contraction, and it won't be something you noticed as stylistically eccentric – but the fact that *I* do it shouldn't be the determining factor in whether I do it *here*. Oftentimes I really shouldn't. Or, indeed, should not. After all, the point of this edit is not to make the book sound more like me, but to make it sound as much as possible like itself. Every paragraph has a moment where, well, *I* certainly wouldn't express myself like that (I'm not sure where that word "oftentimes" came from a few lines up, it's definitely not one of mine); or *I* wouldn't shape a sentence in that way; or *I* wouldn't emphasise this word rather than that word – but I need firmly to resist changing all these things. I'm not trying to make this translation sound like all my other translations, I want it to be as distinct as the original is. So I need to produce what instinctively feels comfortable, and I need to trust my ear – <u>but not too much</u>. That "normal" at the end of the last paragraph should be a terrible warning. It is difficult to avoid the tyranny of that "normal", but it's essential.

When the author writes "he operated the light switch", it's phrased very deliberately, so I must resist the temptation to say "he turned on the light". She uses unusual words, or common words in slightly unusual ways. She describes the detachment of the police force using the word "frigid" rather than "cool" or "detached", so I need to resist the temptation to lapse into one of those easier, less obtrusive alternatives. These things will be an issue at the editorial stage, when whoever edits the book will need to be mindful that these strange choices are deliberate because the book is – at least by the measure of my own everyday prose style – *not quite normal*.

So much for the generalities. For ease of reading, I'm breaking this entry into two – a big specific example from this reading stage will be the focus of the next entry.

5 April (2)

First Read II (This Time It's Particular)

This extract, chosen more or less at random, is page 97 of my printed-out draft, coming a little over halfway through the book. The narrator is visiting a very frail old man at his home to give him a bath. Remember that this is the not-at-all-good first draft that I've just read for the first time, so don't expect too much! Have a read through the text itself, and then look at what I did to it in this week's first reading.

There's something funny going on with the preposition here – between? I sort of know what she's getting at, but the idea of the blurry face being somehow contained *within* the contracting grimace doesn't come across. Would simply *with* the massive grimace be better?

*He's crying. Like every Thursday he has started to cry and his face blurs **between** the massive grimace squeezing it. I take one of the paper tissues and dry his tears. He is sobbing openly, standing up, naked, his arms hanging limp at his sides. Fearful that he might totter and*

There are just too many little words here. All those serial monosyllables, that's just messy. At my first attempt, I try removing a couple of words to make "take hold of him" into "hold him", but I don't like the sound of hold/shoulders, so I remove the second half of the verb phrase instead and settle on just "take him by the shoulders".

No, I don't soak it in the soak. I soak it in the *soap*. Obviously.

Really? Making their way rapidly towards? I believe the word is "approaching".

---

fall, **I take hold of him by the shoulders.**

We're just going to have a quick bath, I say, nice and quick.

No, no, he says.

But **I can see how he is giving way** *and allowing me to help him with his legs. First one, then the other. I check the temperature of the water. I sit him on his bath seat, ready for* **his** *washing. The water is warm, bountiful. I soak the sponge in the* **soak** *and proceed to run it over his chest. I see how thin he's become as his ribs are marked out clearly on his skin,* **betokening** *the exact dimension of his skeleton. I soap his genitals and I can't stop myself looking for a moment at his legs that barely exist anymore* **making their way rapidly towards** *a dangerous undernourishment.*

I squat down so

That's likewise very bitty. Why not just *I can see him giving way now*?

I think "the" works better here than "his". I'll probably change my mind about this half a dozen more times.

I like the idea behind this observation, that she sees his protruding ribs and this somehow sort of predicts the look of his skeleton because he's clearly not long for this world. I don't know about the word "betokens", though. It's there because it's a word I enjoy, but I think it probably sticks out, rib-like, more than it ought to. I might have to do some killing-of-darlings, alas.

This word is still in Spanish all over the manuscript. As I mentioned a couple of weeks ago, it recurs often in the book and I haven't decided exactly what it is in this context. An overall of sorts, more than an apron, I think. I'll need to make a call on this at some point, and then drop the chosen word in to the dozen or so places where I've currently got this placeholder.

I don't like *takes over* here. *Consumes*, perhaps? Typically when translating a Romance language into English, I'll mostly replace Latinate verbs with simpler English phrasal verbs (people *come back* rather than *return*, they *come down* rather than *descend*, *do away with* rather than *eliminate*, etc.); but there are many cases in this book where I'm not doing this (I've reinstated a "return" on p.66, replaced a "holding back" with a "retaining" on p. 70, etc.). It's a combination of being eager to preserve some of the Latinate diction from the original and just aiming for simple economy. I have nothing at all against phrasal verbs (I say this to reassure my friend Ben, if he's reading – a big phrasal-verbs fan is Ben...), it's just that this is very tightly packed prose in Spanish, and turning each one-word verb into a little phrase reduces the density. See also the sprawl I dealt with similarly in the bottom-left comment on the page opposite.

*I can reach his feet with the sponge. The water scatters when it strikes the cap and the plastic of the **DELANTAL** covering me. And **that is** the moment he lifts his leg. His knee hits me full in the face. A blow on such a scale that I experience a universal explosive sensation in the bone of my nose. I fall. Laboriously I sit up on the bathroom floor. There on the ground I press my nose with both hands in an indescribable pain. I curl up. The pain climbs until it **takes over** my head and encloses me or blinds me while I rock back and forth to lessen it, to dislodge the hatred that passes in parallel to moments or minutes waiting surrendered to thousands or millions of*

I'm going for "that's" here rather than "that is". There are many cases where I'm avoiding it, because it doesn't always work with the tone of the narrator's voice, but this one feels like a pretty clear-cut case for me. This sentence describes an abrupt, shocking moment, and I want it to be quick. By contracting, we reach the moment of impact (literally, in this case) one syllable faster. Hmm, maybe I could even replace "the moment" with "when"? *And that's when* rather than *And that is the moment*?

Not *decrease* here: *abate*. I mean, *decrease* is fine, but this is surely one of those phrases the lovely word *abate* was made for, and if I'm not going to use it here, when will I ever?

I prefer "as" here rather than "while", because… Actually I don't know why, but, well, this is my translation and I can do what I like. So there.

*piercing darts, praying for the pain to **decrease**, squeezing my nose. It moves about, expands, intensifies in some areas. I remain like this, sitting on the floor, **reduced to a suffering frag-ment of bones** until I realise how the condensation of the pain is starting to slip away, yes, its power is decreasing **while** the chaotic reality of the water rises up before me.*

I'm sure "reduced to a suffering fragment of bones" meant something when I was drafting this, but I'm damned if I know what. My manuscript has a red **[chk]** written very firmly next to this. It may be that I'll look at the original and discover that this is indeed exactly what it intends, but whatever it's doing clearly isn't working in English just yet. Needs attention.

Tomorrow, as I said, I'll be making these 13 changes to this page, and probably a roughly similar number to each of the manuscript's other 167 pages. Then I'll print it out and start it again.

Even with these changes, the page is very far from anything I'd be ready to show a publisher – let alone a reader – but it is at least inching slowly in the right direction…

7 *April*

Another Status Report, with Numbers

I've incorporated all my edits from the first read, and dealt with some of the many persistent trouble-makers in the text, and the next version is on paper again, ready to read next week.

One of the things I did before printing it out this time around was to check the consistency of certain recurring words. I mentioned a couple of weeks ago that there are quite a few words (a lot of verbs, specially) that recur very many times, mostly used figuratively, all over the book, and I needed to find a translation for each one that could likewise be used in a single recurring form in all those instances. It's not absolutely essential that the same word is *always* translated by the same word in every case, but because I think Diamela's repeated usages are part of the deliberate texture of her Spanish prose, I'd like her <u>English</u> prose to have the same effect wherever I can achieve it. So *entregarse* is now (almost) always *surrender*, *desencadenarse* is *to be unleashed* (doesn't always quite work, but I'm getting there with this one...), *desalojar* is *dislodge*, *traspasar* is *pierce through* and *invadir* is *assail* (not *invade*). *Engranaje* would most commonly be translated as *gears*, but for this book, in most cases I'm going with *mechanism*.

(There are a few as yet unresolved: e.g. *las bases* appears many times, but in context it could be something like *the foundational/basic rules* or it could mean the militant party's *rank and file*. I'm sure it means the same every time, but which?)

Some numbers for you:

The previous draft was 48,929 words long. The edit generated a net loss of 327 words, so it's currently 48,602 words and falling. The word "that" alone makes 28 fewer appearances.

(And because I'm sure this is just the kind of thing you're desperate to know, the word-count thus far for this diary is 25,553.)

The manuscript (it feels a bit grand to be calling it a "manuscript" already, doesn't it?) also contains 176 asterisks. There's an asterisk marking each thing about which I still have a specific doubt – a word I'm using but about which I'm still uncertain, one of the few remaining words/phrases still in Spanish, a note to myself to check something. I find this a useful way of making sure I don't miss anything, and the asterisks are searchable, of course. Over the coming weeks, along with the reading and rereading and rerereading, I'll be making sure each of these gets resolved. That number should keep dropping as I progress; when I do a search of the document and find that it contains no asterisks, well, then I'll have arrived.

So: the newly printed draft.

The line spaces are smaller this time – each time I read through the book, there should be less that it requires doing to it, so I no longer need the lines to be massively spaced to allow for quite so much scribbling.

This means we're now at a pleasingly compact 133 pages, down from the previous 168.

I'll be reading this draft through from start to finish next week. By the end of the week there should be fewer than 176 asterisks, I suspect slightly fewer than 48,602 words, and some marginally better-crafted prose. At some point along the way, I'll share a single paragraph as it has appeared at several developmental stages, for you to see the (I hope) progress.

But for today, just one more task, and it's a small but significant one. It's time to write to The Author.

9 April

A brief question has come in from a reader, responding to Monday's post, about contractions, asking whether their use or otherwise shouldn't be consistent. (The assumption is that the reader comes to expect the narrator to speak in a particular way, over the course of the book.)

Personally, I don't think consistency across the whole narrative is important when you're talking about something like contractions, so long as what's produced doesn't feel like an incoherent voice, but like a coherent voice that just maybe is not always consistent – the latter is how most of us use language when we talk, isn't it? (Like that "doesn't… is not" sentence I've just written.) This slightly distant-seeming narrative will certainly have a lot of uncontracted verbs, as long as the rhythm works for me, but that same voice might contract more when she's addressing someone directly – but even in direct speech she still might choose sometimes not to contract for greater emphasis. ("I will not contract my verbs, do you hear me? I just won't do it.") Again, that kind of "inconsistency" is something we English-users do all the time. Don't think I'm going to worry about this one.

11 April

Iterations

As I work through the second full read, I thought it might be worth giving some sense of the overall process thus far. So here, at various evolutionary stages, is a paragraph from about a quarter of the way into the book.

First the Spanish original, for those of you for whom it might be of any interest:

> *Me desplazo por el pasillo mientras me afirmo sucesi-vamente en los metales. Mi cuerpo no deja de sacudirse. Sólo cuando el bus se detiene por completo, desciendo y pongo con cautela mis pies en la acera. Nadie más que yo se ha bajado hoy en este paradero. Llevo en la mente el número de calles que debo atravesar, cinco. Sí, cinco, pienso, a la vez que imprimo un ritmo parejo a cada uno de mis pasos. Rápido. Hoy me acosa el viento helado de la mañana. Tendré que soportar este frío prematuro para llegar hasta la casa donde me esperan.*

Then that first draft (honestly, I still can't believe I'm even showing you this rubbish):

I ME DESPLAZO POR [move along/down?] the corridor while I ME AFIRMO EN the metals [los metales] successively [in turn?]. My body doesn't stop shaking. Only when the bus stops completely, I get out and tentatively [con cautela] put my feet onto the ACERA [pvt/sdwk]. Nobody but me has got out today at this stop. In my mind I have the number of streets I have to cross, five of them. Yes, five, I think, A LA VEZ QUE I IMPRIMO an even rhythm to each of my steps. Quick. Today the freezing morning wind ACOSA me. I'll have to put up with this premature cold to arrive at the house where they are waiting for me.

Then, a couple of weeks ago, after looking things up, making some choices:

I move down the corridor while I steady myself on the metal bars★ in turn. My body doesn't stop shaking. Only when the bus stops completely, and I get out and tentatively put my feet onto the pavement. Nobody but me has got out today at this stop. In my mind I have the number of streets I have to cross, five of them. Yes, five, I think, while I imprint an even rhythm to each of my steps. Quick. Today the freezing morning wind is harrying me. I'll have to put up with this premature cold to arrive at the house where they are waiting for me.

Last week, after I'd completed the first full read of the translation:

I move down the aisle, steadying myself on the metal bars in turn. My body doesn't stop shaking. Not until the bus stops completely, and I get out and tentatively [gingerly?] put my feet onto the pavement. Nobody but me has got out today at this stop. In my mind I have

*the number of streets I have to cross, five of them. Yes,
five, I think, while I imprint an even rhythm onto each
of my steps. Quick. Today there's a freezing morning
wind harrying me. I'll have to put up with this premature cold to arrive at the house where I'm expected.*

And now, after the second full read:

*I move down the aisle, steadying myself on the metal bars
in turn. My body doesn't stop shaking. Not until the bus
comes to a complete halt, and I step out carefully onto the
pavement. Nobody but me has got off here/at this one
[at this stop] today. In my mind I'm holding the number
of streets I have to cross, five of them. Yes, five, I think, as
I imprint an even rhythm onto each of my steps. Quickly
now. Today there's an icy morning wind harrying me. I'm
going to have to put up with this premature cold to arrive
at the house where I'm expected.*

Getting there? You know, I think we just might be...

P.S. (1) The reason those "metal bars" took a little while to
resolve: it's obvious from the context what the meaning
is (the narrator's holding on to something metal to stop
herself falling while on a moving bus), but I realised
that the same word – *metales* – is used again on the very
next page to describe whatever it is that the frail old
lady holds onto in order to keep herself upright when
standing in the bathroom. Because I don't think any of
Diamela's word choices are careless, I want to make the
same connection between the parallel scenes in English
as she does in Spanish, so I needed to use a term that
could work for both scenarios.

P.S. (2) The reason for the "got off here" or "got off at this one" in the latest version, in place of the "at this stop": the verb "stop" used to appear in the previous sentence, *and* in the one before that, so I'm trying to avoid also using the noun "stop" here, though realistically I know I might just end up restoring it at some point. (Hence also the change to "complete halt".) I might also have to lose that annoyingly similar "step", I guess, though I do like "step out" here.

P.S. (3) The reason I'm keeping "In my mind I'm holding…": that's one of those cases where I have to resist the temptation to normalise Diamela's unusual framing of a sentence or an idea. It would be tempting to edit this into, say, "I'm thinking about", but that's not quite the same thing. "In my mind I have" is weirder, but better, and I'll keep it if I think I can get away with it…

P.S. (4) Ah, I'm rather sorry not to be able to use "gingerly". Such a nice old word.

15 April

A few interesting suggestions today from Daniel S., who refers to my "layered, systematic approach", though he guesses – quite rightly – that "there's a healthy amount of creative chaos involved as well". He writes specifically about that first sentence, the one about swaying down the aisle of a moving bus:

> *"Me desplazo por el pasillo mientras ME AFIRMO sucesivamente en los METALES."*
>
> *The use of "afirmar" in the reflexive to indicate physical support is correct but not common; usually it connotes a more emotional or psychological aspect of affirmation. So I get the sense that she is steadying herself both physically & emotionally for what's to come.*
>
> *Additionally, I think the imprecision of saying "metales" rather than "barras de metal" is deliberate, as "metales" increases the sensorial experience. She just sees the substance, the raw material. It's almost like she is part of this organism that is the bus. I could be reading too much into this, and it's maybe just her Chilean "modismos" or the fact that I'm reading the passage out of context, but the first sentence seemed to have a bigger sensorial impact in the Spanish version.*

Yes, I think Dan's right – the narrator is reporting that she's steadying herself in a physical sense – the bus is rocking, she doesn't want to fall – but we also get the idea of her just sort of bracing herself for the task ahead. "Steadying myself" can thus be deliberately vague (rather than holding on "to try to keep my balance" or similar).

And yeah, as he has spotted, the "metales" is a problem. Because the focus is on the material rather than the form it takes, the Spanish does make you feel the contact of skin on metal much more. I was toying with the idea of just "metal" in the singular – *steadying myself on the metal*, which would work for the iteration on the next page, too – but it does somehow need to convey the sense of a number of different things, in the plural, each of them touched "in turn".

Dan's message also suggests trying to work in the phrasal verb "call to mind" – i.e. "I call the number of streets to mind…" – which is an option I hadn't thought of, and it's a good one. But it would be slightly less elegant phrasing in my context than the way Dan suggested it, because the object isn't just "the streets" or "the number of streets" but "the number of streets I have to cross", and that phrase can't really be split very easily, which means going with either "I call to mind the number of streets I have to cross" or "I call the-number-of-streets-I-have-to-cross to mind" – the former preferable but still a little sprawly. What bothers me more about the phrase, though, is that I don't believe she's actively *deciding* to summon up that number and think about it, I think it's just there, present in her mind, whether she likes it or not. So having/holding does that better, I think. Not that I think the current solution sounds quite right, but it's a not-sounding-quite-right that I happen not to mind in this instance!

19 April

Many, Many Small Things

First of all, my apologies in advance: this is going to be a long and very fragmentary, bits-and-pieces sort of entry. We're approaching the end of the whole process (!) and there are so many little things I want to remember to mop up before finishing. Next entry will be more substantial and more coherent. But this will have to do for now.

So...

After a few days' unexpected delay, I'm finally nearing the end of the second full read. As you saw with the evolving paragraph I shared last week, we're approaching something readable, slowly but surely. I started to get a good sense of the book's rhythms, that intense, looping voice, from that first pass (as well as the author's politics, the very deliberate way she reshapes language, etc.); so while the second read has thrown up ten million things I still want to change (well, approximately. I haven't done an exact count), they are at least mostly *small* things.[30] So here's some of the stuff I've found in this iteration and tried to deal with.

1: "Or else you read, yes, you read, with a remarkable focus that captivates me, you read in the middle of the difficulty caused by the inadequate size of the letters. You read without seeing…"

I'm adding two words to the opening phrase of the sentence: "or else you *sit and* read". Why? Because without it some people will understand it as being "read" in the present tense (reed) and others as "read" in the past tense (red), and I need to be sure they know it's the former. While a lot of the book does jump about in time, sometimes within a single sentence, in this case the Spanish verb isn't even momentarily ambiguous, so the English shouldn't be if I can help it. (Whether the character in question is actually *sitting* to do his reading, I don't know. I'm guessing. No harm done, I think.)

2: Pronouns are a constant problem. Spanish can often do without them in places where English cannot, leading to sequences of verbs that acquire annoying repetitions in their translation.

Look at this Spanish text – even if you don't know the language, you'll see there is no conspicuous repetition:

> *Vuelvo a la mesa y a mi silla. Olvido, sí, intento olvidar mis dedos sobre el arroz, recogiendo los granos húmedos, me limpio los dedos en la falda y entonces, en un gesto decidido, cierro el cuaderno. Voy hasta la cama, me*

---

[30] At a later stage in the process, Bill, the book's editor, would refer to one sentence as sounding "like a badly tuned radio"; and there's a lot of that to be fixed at this stage. Sentences that are, you know, *sort of* there, but there's just a little bit of annoying interference to be eliminated…

siento en la orilla. Espero iniciar contigo un intercambio
pacífico que me permita…

The English, however, has no fewer than eight "I"s:

I go back to the table and to my chair. I forget, yes, I try
to forget my fingers on the rice, gathering up the damp
grains, I wipe my fingers on my skirt and then, deci-
sively, I shut the notebook. I go over to the bed, I sit on
the edge. I wait to begin a peaceful exchange with you
that will allow me to…

Cases like these are among the few situations in
which I regularly combine previously separate sentences,
just to avoid this new and annoying repetition. E.g.: "I
go over to the bed, sit on the edge, and wait to begin a
peaceful…". Not too terrible, I think. Or here's another:

I straighten her up, and put on her nightie. I open the
nightstand and take out the small brush. I comb her
hair, taking care to disentangle the strands gently, then
I lie her back down, arrange the sheets, smooth the
bedcover and position the pillows beneath her head…

You'll notice I've already avoided a lot of I's in that
latter part – eliding *I* arrange, *I* smooth, *I* position. *I, I,*
I…[31] Maybe I could also avoid the third sentence starting
with an "I" by doing something like "<u>*As*</u> I comb her hair,
taking…"[32]

---

[31] *Ay, ay, ay… (Ed.)*

[32] This came up in a comment from Marina a while back, who reported
that she has the same issue with Romanian, since subjects "are of course
obvious from verb forms in Romance languages, but can quickly sound
extremely repetitive or egocentric in English (even where that is not at
all the case in the original)."

3: I've mentioned before that prepositions are a problem. The word "ante" appears 58 times in the novel, and can be variously *faced with*, *before*, *at*, or other things entirely.

The characters are very frequently lying either *in* the bed, or *on* the bed, and often only context can tell me which. There's one case, for example, where the narrator sees the other character lying on [?] the bed, but later in the scene refers to spotting him out the corner of her eye as just this sort of shapeless lump – and so I then pictured him as being curled up *under* the covers, hence went back and changed my previous uncertain "on" to a firm "in".

(While on the subject of that bed: this is a book set in one small room where the characters are locked down for ages – imagine that![33] – just moving occasionally to the kitchen or bathroom and then back again, and the room in question has only a bed and a table and a chair. As a result, the bed, that particular piece of furniture in the small room, looms large in the characters' lives. Which is why, somewhat unusually, I've tended to go with *lying in the bed* rather than just *lying in bed*. That night, I tossed and turned in *the* bed, etc.)

When the narrator places her hand on the wall and slips her fingertips POR its surface, she is running them over it, or across it – or perhaps up it? Down it? Along it? I'd quite like to be more precise than just "over" in English, but I've no way of knowing with any certainty from the Spanish which direction the fingers are moving in. Does it matter? Honestly, probably not. But there's a point in every translation process where it feels like *everything* has to matter a great deal and frankly I can't wait till I've got past it.

---

[33] Topical reference to Covid-19 lockdown restrictions prevailing at the time of the diary's composition. *(Ed.)*

4: One of the secondary characters who's referred to occasionally, a former fellow militant, goes by the name Lucho. *Lucho* is a common diminutive of the common name *Luis*. However, it is also a verb, meaning *I fight/ struggle*, and it's used in this way elsewhere in the book. If I keep his name as it is, the English reader won't see the connection. I'm sure there's a clever solution, but I haven't got it yet. Maybe tomorrow.

5: The phrase "on this occasion, possessed by" has become "on this occasion, possessed *as I was* by". The Spanish tells you that the possessed refers to the narrator because the word is gendered (see also my entry on February 8), so I need to smuggle in a few extra words to do that. (This is an even more frequent problem in Portuguese where a simple "thank you" reveals a speaker's gender. Maddening language.)

6: The line "a century that ended almost unnoticed, with no glory" would be just fine, except that the idiom used in the Spanish for "unnoticed" is "sin pena ni gloria", which includes "without glory" within it, so one attribute seems somehow to contain the other. So I need to connect them. I'm toying currently with "a century that ended almost unremarked, and unremarkable".

(That's rather nice, actually. Well done me.)

7: I want to err on the side of economy for this book. Going for sentences with density rather than sprawl. This means sometimes using a single chunky Latinate word rather than a phrase made up of several shorter Anglo-Saxon ones (as in the phrasal verb examples I talked about in the second entry on April 5). The slightly more-Latinate-than-usual language works here anyway, I think.

But…

My fervent economy drive doesn't extend to removing the articles for *the* bed (point 3, above); and I'm still wavering about whether to cut things like these italicised words:

That's what you tell me, and I obey *you*.
You're looking well, I say *to her*.
Time for us to get dressed, I say *to him*.

In almost any other translation, I'd cut these words with hardly a thought – it's very common for Spanish to testify explicitly to the intended recipient of every bit of dialogue in a way that we don't usually in English. From the context – a conversation in which we know there are only two people involved – there's really no possible ambiguity. But this book is so much about these two people, and their relationship, and the ways in which their lives blur into one, and how she treats him and how he treats her and what she said to him and what he did to her, it somehow seems as though keeping these explicit, almost annoyingly repetitive little markers has some value.

Some of the economy will come in contractions, but as I mentioned on the 5th, these won't always work for this voice. The prose is perfectly digestible, it isn't obstructive, but casual it ain't. So while I'm contracting where I can – usually where it feels more like direct speech – I do need to keep fully uncontracted verbs (am not, do not, cannot) much of the time.

8: On April 7, I listed a few of the text's little linguistic tics (wow, that's got to be a hard phrase to say out loud – N.B.: fix this before we make the audiobook) – those words or phrases that recur in the Spanish and which I want to have similarly recurring in my translation. There's another little tic I might mention: in the translation, the narrator refers to things emphatically as "so, so very…" – e.g. "I look over to the bed, and you're so, so very curled up". The formulation appears so, so many times in my manuscript, because Diamela has something similarly recurrent in hers. Always got to be on the lookout for these habits that need replicating.

9: As I've mentioned before, the translation needs to function more or less across the English-speaking world. But it's not just a translation into a multicontinental language, it's also a translation *from* one – in this case I'm translating to British-ish English, from the Spanish of a specifically Chilean novelist. Hence my care in checking that handy little book of Chilean-specific words and phrases I bought for the purpose. There's almost nothing culturally to identify the book as Chilean (so almost nothing that needs surreptitiously explaining to my readers, those early *frentistas* notwithstanding), so any potential Chile specifics are just about language use and vocabulary. But the risk for me isn't coming across a Chilean word I've never seen before – I can always look that up if I do, that's easy enough; no, the risk is seeing a word I think I know, I *assume* I know, but not realising that the Chilean usage is different. It's those unknown unknowns again. There are still a few possible words about which I have my doubts. (I have been meaning to write a separate entry on Englishes and Spanishes, but I can't do everything. I keep being distracted by too much other trouble in this book…).

10: I'm still struggling with the strange references to some kind of "judge" in a legal system I can't quite under-stand, in relation to car accidents. In a conversation with a group of friends last week about one of their ongoing translations, the phrase "investigatory magistrate" came up, and I might steal that term for mine. Not perfect, but better than anything else I've got currently.

11: Following my doubt expressed two weeks ago, I'm definitely going with the word "purpose" for "destino", rather than the usual "destiny" or "destination". Spanish-language writers frequently take advantage of the ambiguity of their word, using it in a way that allows for a more or less figurative reading – but in English, inevitably, I have to choose. "We had become a cell with no purpose" – *purpose* is not quite one thing nor the other, but I reckon better than either of the more usual translations available here.

12: As I mentioned a few weeks ago, the word "bread" was causing me trouble. Fortunately I happened to mention this the other day to my friend James who used to live in Chile, and after a couple of minutes on Google Images, I think he might have solved my problem.

13 to 48602: All the other words have loads of stuff going on, too. Today is the sort of day when it feels like not one of them is totally easy.

And yet, it will be over, and strangely soon. All this finicky business above notwithstanding, I should, at my current pace, finish this read-through tomorrow.

Then I will send it – the whole draft translation, doubts and all – to the author.

And then wait.

21 April

A postscript to point 10: thanks to some insight from my Chilean stepdad, the mystery of that difficult "judge" word has been solved!

Only 48,601 to go.

22 April

What Next?

This elusive little book is nearly within my grasp, I think.

I've finished my second read-through, and I've incorporated all my little scribbles into the Word document. The manuscript is currently 48,418 words long (which means it's slimmed down by about 200 more words over the course of this reading); and there are 153 outstanding doubts, each marked with an asterisk.

And that's the version I have just e-mailed to the author.

I'm going to look away from the book now for at least a couple of weeks, and then return to it with slightly fresher eyes. And in the meantime, it should have arrived in the author's inbox about an hour ago, for her to do with it as she pleases while I'm off-duty. I know she's very busy, so I don't want to make great demands of her, but I want her at least to have the option of looking at the translation and commenting if she feels she would like to, and it makes sense for that to happen during this fallow period while I won't be fiddling with it myself.

On Monday, I shared a few examples of the sorts of little things I did in this second read. A lot of the other small changes were matters of rhythm, and I'll be doing more on that when I return to the book after this hiatus. I also spent more time than is probably reasonable struggling with verbs of laughter, which are <u>weirdly difficult</u> to translate from Spanish into plausible English. On the plus side, only today I worked out a rather nifty little bit of wordplay balancing the words "trouble" and "rubble", which was pleasing; and somewhere else referred to a character's feeling of *edginess* caused by being in pain, and then popping a painkiller *to take the edge off* – a nice little effect delightfully gained in translation.

Several of my other entries have referred to this novel's ambiguities, and these are an area of which I tried to be particularly mindful in this latest reading. Diamela very deliberately blurs the boundaries between one character and another; she slips between timeframes sometimes within a single sentence, between literal and figurative, between highly physical representations and seemingly disembodied ones; and crucial bits of narrative clarification are entirely absent, so you might be inclined to speculate about what happened (who actually died when?), but those crucial facts are not always in sharp focus.

Some of the author's ambiguity is on a sentence-structure level, too. Have a look, for example, at this: *The man who's critically injured is breathing lightly sinking into unconsciousness.* If that were my sentence (or perhaps I should say, if it were *only* mine), I would want to put a comma in for clarification – because what exactly is happening *lightly* here? As it stands, you might read it as the man *breathing lightly* while *sinking…*; or you might read it as *breathing* while *lightly sinking…* The Spanish allows for both – I must resist the temptation to narrow it to my own preferred interpretation.

(At the same time, of course, I have to be on the lookout for <u>unintended</u> ambiguities in the translation.

One of my sentences used to begin *I look at the slippers, sitting on the edge of the bed*, and I changed the *sitting* to *as I sit* to avoid the possibility that you might understand it to mean that the *slippers* are sitting on the edge of the bed. That ambiguity does not exist in the Spanish, so I'm eager to banish the possibility from mine. Diamela has more than enough ambiguities of her own for me to start adding silly new ones.)

This constant instability in the original, this constant play of ambiguities, requires a particular effort not to inadvertently clarify: if it's not clear in the original which of two possible characters is being referred to, say, I must be careful not to have the translation specify. In some cases this makes my job easier – I actively need *not* to choose which interpretation to make, and, well, at least this saves me the trouble of choosing. More often than not, though, keeping options open in the translation is a challenge. Not infrequently it involves editing and editing and editing and ultimately ending up with the simplest translation, closest to the original, that frankly I should have used to begin with.

(A group of us were workshopping a title for a friend's book last week, and the same thing happened: after lots of trying-to-be-clever on our part, it became clear that simply translating the original title, pretty much as it was, would actually produce the best result. Naturally, the solution will seem so obvious to a reader that they'll have no idea how much interim work had to be put into the problem to arrive apparently-nowhere-at-all.)

While tinkering my way through this second read, I've had to admit defeat in two places. One is a conversation where, in the original Spanish, you don't know which character is being discussed, because there are no markers of the subject's gender, an effect that cleverly compromises your experience when you're reading; and one is the problem I referred to on Monday, about a character whose name (well, actually his undercover alias) also functions as an active verb in Spanish – another bit of deliberate blurring. I've had to give both of these up for lost causes, and simply accept that the problems I was facing were not things to which I was ever going to find a solution. Which I *hate* to do.

Still, those two examples of failure notwithstanding,[34] after this second reading I think I've mostly got the ambiguities where I want them. (And not where I don't.) A lot of what will come next, when I'm back at the novelface next month, will be reading for sound, and rhythm, and density. The meaning is basically sorted; the actual reading <u>experience</u> (which of course includes meaning but also very much more than that) is nearly there, but not quite. A couple of weeks of clearing my head with other work, and other reading, will allow me to launch myself back into Never-Never-land with an attitude that's a bit more like that of an uncompromised reader. I've been working on this book on and off for nearly three months now (my first entry in this diary was late January), so I'm currently in a bit too deep. Time to step away, and take a few deep breaths.

~~In the meantime, since we're approaching the end of this process, if there are things you think I should write about in the few remaining entries, or questions you'd like answered, do please ask and I'll make sure to cover everything before I bring this all to a close.~~ [35]

Right, then – back in a couple of weeks…

P.S. Tonight I managed to incorporate the word "hoick" into the translation, which made me happy. It's a word I like, and which vaguely amuses me. I have no earthly idea why.

---

[34] I would in fact return to half-solve one of these a little later. Bloody-mindedness is a valuable quality in late drafts.

[35] Nope – too late! *(Ed.)*

23 April

On Englishes

I've had a reminder from Elena about the matter of different country-specific Englishes and Spanishes, which I've promised to write about but never got round to.

Well, in this instance, the variations in Spanish are less of a problem than the English. The author of the book is Chilean, but there are relatively few cases of Chilean-specific words and usages, and I happen to know enough Chileans to recognise these when they appear. (An obvious one: a "guagua" appears as a baby, from time to time.) The idiosyncrasies of Diamela's prose are not rooted in its Chilean-ness, nor in the friction between different kinds of Spanish, so in fact this proved not to be much of an issue in translating it. (Compare this to a novel by Juan Pablo Villalobos that I recently translated, which features characters from several different Spanish-speaking countries, all talking quite differently and even drawing attention to these differences. Now *that's* hard.)

English is more of a problem, simply because this translation is going to be published across the Anglosphere in a single edition, and has to work for readers in Detroit or Dublin just as well as readers in Newcastle. Most of this translation is using "my" English – more about which in a moment – but there's a risk that what feels like my "neutral" is also a Britishness that will jar for readers elsewhere (these characters aren't British, so why do they sound it?). And there's a risk, too, that it will sound simply awkward to those readers furthest away from me. A lot of the time, the difference between Englishes isn't a matter of obvious vocabulary – cookies and mobiles and so on – but of rhythm and small prepositions and things that are harder to pin down. (I remember a review many years ago that quoted a couple of phrases from my translation of a Brazilian novel to illustrate how "unnatural" they were, despite their being in fact entirely idiomatic – but while they were totally commonplace usages to me, I hadn't realised they were also UK-specific, and were phrases that I suspect the reviewer, in this case from the US, simply hadn't come across before.)

My own English is mostly British, and it's from 2021, and it's of a Londoner in his 40s. But that's only a part of it, because my idiolect – my own particular collection of language habits – will be unique to me, of course. And the divide is much less blunt than merely British English vs Indian English vs Australian English etc. My language use has all kinds of influences that are not only contemporary and local; and I have things I like and things I don't. Even when writing for English publications, I tend to follow the North American habit of ending words in -ize rather than -ise; even when I'm not translating in an American accent, I err on the side of cellphones rather than mobiles. I go to watch movies more often than films. This particular translation has a lovely "outwith" in it – even as a non-Scot, I don't see a problem with that. In some cases, having an editor with an English sufficiently different from yours can be helpful, as they stumble over things that are so local as to confuse them, but it's not, ultimately, a solvable problem. Nor, indeed, is it a "problem" at all, exactly. No person's language is neutral, fortunately, and we have to make choices (as I've mentioned, in this translation I have *diapers* rather than *nappies*, but *pavements* rather than *sidewalks*); not being afraid of using our own particular resources, but also remaining aware of what implications those choices will have for our infinitely various potential readers.

1 May

Tough Sentences

I've been spending some of this fortnight, while the Diamela novel is paused, working on the first draft of another book, also a translation from Spanish. And after a couple of months spent attempting to wrangle *Never Did the Fire*, this other book is so easy!

(So it turns out that I am sometimes capable of translating, after all. It's quite reassuring, if I'm honest.)

The contrast has made me think about what it is that makes Diamela's book <u>not</u> easy. Some of it I've talked about in other entries – the persistent ambiguities discussed on April 22, for instance. Also, the movement of each sentence is so controlled that recreating that trajectory in a language where natural word-order is necessarily different can be incredibly tricky.[36] Spanish and English are not all that structurally different in comparison to many language pairs, but even the relatively small discrepancies cause trouble when the author is using every little micro-

---

[36] It occurs to me that perhaps this specific combination – great precision of prose with significant, deliberate blurriness in the effect – might be the hardest thing of all to pull off, for writer as well as translator.

resource her language allows her. Then there are the internal echoes, there's the curiously hard-to-pin-down narrative voice, and there's the density of the prose – every word with a lot of weight, unnecessary words omitted.

It's not easy to explain. But I wonder whether looking at a single sentence might help to convey how these problems all pile up. So I open the book at random. Page 80. Here, for Spanish-speakers and non-Sp-sp alike, is a fairly standard sentence from *Jamás el fuego nunca*. It's referring to the latest militant cell with which the narrator has become involved. (If you know Spanish, you'll see at a glance that it isn't especially mysterious.)

Los diez cuerpos batallábamos frente a las dificultades, sabíamos que estábamos rodeados por otras células, perseguidos, involucrados en nuestras chapas.

And now here it is again, in bits:

Los diez cuerpos
The ten bodies
> [OK, that bit actually is totally easy. Look up each of these three words in turn in a Spanish-English dictionary, and there's your answer: *The. Ten. Bodies.*]

batallábamos
battled
> [*Batallar* means *To battle*. But here the form of the verb is the first person plural – in other words, it means *we battled*. Those ten bodies at the start of the sentence are still the subject, though, so having thought the opening of the sentence was all set, I need to loop back to change the opening subject from *The ten bodies* to *We ten bodies*. So: *We ten*

bodies battled. But I wonder if "were battling" might be better – it's definitely not a single action in the Spanish, it's continuous, and maybe the English should do the same? *We ten bodies were battling*?]

frente a
faced with

[This is one of those wretched prepositions I referred to on April 19. It can mean "in front of" in a literal, physical sense, or figuratively – something like "faced with".[37] The latter is what I think is happening here: they are doing battle in the face of something-or-other. It's worth noting, though, that the author/narrator has specifically chosen to use *frente* here, and repeatedly elsewhere, rather than one of several possible alternatives – and *frente* is a word that also means "front" in the sense of a political movement, just like the English usage. Judean People's Front, Popular People's Front of Judea, and so on.[38] I don't know whether the effect is intended, and in any other text I'd assume the connection was entirely irrelevant, but given that this is a book in part about small sectarian political movements, this recurring term needs thought. Remember way back on February 1 where the narrator was called a "frentista"? So that word carries a lot of weight. Are we really supposed to not notice all the *frentes* after that? Yes, "faced with" seems more natural in this context, but it loses that political-movement resonance entirely.]

---

[37] The opening line of *One Hundred Years of Solitude* sees a man "frente a" a firing squad. The translator Gregory Rabassa didn't use a preposition at all, just recast it with a verb: "*As he faced* the firing squad...". One of the many things that makes the sentence brilliant.

[38] Splitters.

[Note, too: there is no punctuation in the Spanish between *battled* and *faced with*. Can I similarly get away without a comma in English? *We ten bodies battled faced with…* The problem is, I think the English is more confusing than the Spanish if left unpunctuated, partly because in English those adjacent words "*battled faced*" look like equivalent parts of speech. I might need to adjust the punctuation after all. *We ten bodied battled, faced with…*]

las dificultades,
the difficulties,

[Or just *difficulties*, without the *the*. As I explained on February 12, this is a recurring question in the Spanish, and in Spanish. It's usually easy to resolve from context, but when you have a piece of writing where even the context is constantly undermining you, the answers aren't always that obvious. Tsk, writers, eh?]

sabíamos que estábamos rodeados por otras células,
we knew that we were surrounded by other cells,

[This is straightforward enough. Though in the interests of economy, I'll probably take out the "that", which is a trace leftover from the Spanish structure but is redundant in reasonably informal English.]

perseguidos,
pursued,

[This could be *pursued* or *persecuted* – I suspect it'll be one of those words I'll keep switching back and forth and only decide at the last moment. *Pursued* has echoes of the hunt, which I like; but I think the political overtones of *persecuted* work here, too. Incidentally, this adjective refers to "we", not to the word immediately preceding it, "cells". The meaning is not *we are surrounded by other cells [that are] pursued*, it's *we are surrounded by other cells [and we are] pursued…*" As you may remember from my 8 February entry, Spanish adjectives agree with their nouns in both gender and number. In this case, the clue is in the last two letters of the word – *os*. If it were describing the cells – which are *células*, a feminine noun – it would be *perseguidas*.]

involucrados en
?? in

[*Involucrados* is the hardest word in the sentence, for my money. It's used as an adjective, it's referring to "we" again – you can tell by those last two letters – and the meaning is something like "involved [in]". If the words that followed were, say, "a cunning plan", then "involved in" might work. But they aren't, rather they relate to the militants' fake names/identities – would *involved in our fake names* mean anything to anyone, really? I don't want a word that's too obvious, because the Spanish isn't doing anything too obvious, but the sense I want to convey is somewhere between involved in, attached to, jumbled/merged together with. I think – *I think* – what the author's getting at is somewhere around there. I'm still a little blurry, though.]

nuestras chapas.
our aliases.

[*Chapas* is a word that was still in Spanish until just a couple of drafts ago – it's *aliases* now. The solution is not quite as obvious as it might seem

in my translation – it's a rarer usage in the original than my common English "alias" suggests;
but the good news is that this isn't the first time it
appears in the book – on page 32, the characters
are described as being *still attached to their last/
latest alias* – so by this point in the translation,
there's a precedent. The decision was embedded
in the text earlier, and it can still stand here.
(And, I hope, consistently in all the many other
instances that follow.)]

So where does that leave us? Well, in the current draft
(the one that's quietly simmering away on its own, and to
which I'll return next week), the sentence reads:

**We ten bodies battled against difficulties, we
knew we were surrounded by other cells, pursued, mixed up in our aliases.**

I think the "against" is too easy a solution, almost
certainly something I just lazily normalised during an
edit. I might revisit that. Otherwise this works for me. The
"mixed up" is nice – conveying both a complicity and
also a complicated messy entanglement. The sentence as a
whole follows the same thought processes as the Spanish,
and at twenty words is just as compact. In fact, it's far
shorter than the original in characters, syllables, etc., so it
doesn't feel like there's any unnecessary sprawl… though
now I'm thinking the rhythm is more clipped – maybe
too clipped? – with all those short Anglo-Saxon words,
compared to all those more substantial Spanish ones, and
I'm not sure I like that. Might need to reconsider. How
about replacing "pursued, mixed up" with "persecuted,
entangled"? That's much more in tune with the feel of
the Spanish. I like the meaning of "entangled" much

less than "mixed up", but I like the rhythm and register rather more.

(Dammit, I wasn't planning to use this entry to do any editing as I'm supposed to be <u>not working on this text now</u>, but it's hard to resist meddling once you're in.)

One general point, before I slip back into my temporary Diamela holiday. I could have used pretty much any decent-length sentence in this book and looked at its parts in this way. I hope it's obvious, however, that what I'm showing today isn't in reality how I usually work! At twenty words, this sentence is one 2,420th of the book. When I've finally got my last composite draft of this sentence done, and I'm sure I'm happy with it, and it's gone through edits and proofs and been magicked into a printed book, it will earn me £1.90, which means that in practical terms, my working process cannot possibly afford my having a diligent little conversation with myself about each individual word, weighing up every pro and con, etc. Which is not to say that the weighing-up doesn't happen, of course, only that typically, much of it isn't conscious or deliberate. Apparently <u>on some level</u> I must have been happier with "pursued" than "persecuted" in this case, even if I didn't stop to think why or to articulate the decision.

That proviso aside, however, this one particular book has certainly obliged me to be a lot more deliberate about my choices, more aware of them, than almost any other I've worked on. Obviously some part of that is down to the process of keeping this diary in parallel, which forces me to examine and articulate what I'm doing in real time (and the experiment is affected by its being observed, of course – in other words, it's partly <u>your fault</u>). But it's also down to the nature of Diamela's writing, which, simply put, has a much higher-than-average number of words that cause me trouble in countless different ways,

177

and hence which snag en route and demand my direct attention. She makes it impossible, then, to be thoughtless. That is why there were even more oh-just-leave-it-in-Spanish-and-figure-it-out-later words in the first draft than I usually allow myself. Of course, the many-layered subtlety of what the original is doing, even on a micro level, is also where its brilliance is to be found. Which raises the stakes for a translator, but it's where the rewards of the job are, too.

Quite looking forward to getting back to it, actually.

4 May

Never-ending?

Just a quick break from my break to answer a question from Sabine, who asks how I know when to stop improving/changing a translation, other than by the presence of a looming deadline.

The truth is, if things are going well, the ending of the process will happen automatically, because each of my many read-throughs will demand fewer changes than the one before. By the time I come to my final pass over the text, I might want to change the odd word/comma every few pages, rather than several things a line. So that's an indication of progress. I don't think I would ever reach a point when I'd read a draft and want to make *zero* changes, but the ever-decreasing number is certainly tending that way. Think of it as the Zeno's Paradox of editorial work.

The point when the pre-delivery tinkering stops is not arbitrary but is at least sort of artificial, and yes, that might well be governed by a deadline. It won't exactly be *finished* then, but that's also because the editorial process allows the refinements to continue even after the deadlined delivery, so I don't *need* to feel it's perfect. Which is just as well.

9 May

The Final Read (Almost)

Well, first things first. I've heard back from the author and she's very happy with the translation. What she saw was not the final version, of course, but close enough that it should be recognisably her book, at least. It was kind of her to take the time to look at it and I'm most grateful – this moment is always a relief. (It matters to me that my authors feel well represented.) She responded to a few dozen specific doubts I had, helping me to find a little clarity, where appropriate. As to the rest, I am reassured that she has now seen the decisions I've been taking, and didn't raise objections.

(She does of course know about this diary, too, so since late January has had ample opportunity to follow all the ghastly things I've been perpetrating on her beautiful novel. At this point, I can only assume that she is unshockable.)

Having set the book aside for a couple of weeks while Diamela was looking at it, I've returned to the manuscript this weekend and read it all straight through, reasonably speedily. The distance is so useful. Even two weeks – some of which I spent churning out the quick first draft of another book that, helpfully, couldn't be more different – was enough for me to tune out of it almost completely. And when I returned to it, two days ago, it didn't take me more than a page or so to think: *I know what this book sounds like, I recognise the writer's rhythms and patterns. I have confidence in the narrator's voice.*

In short: *I think it works.*

The reading did still throw up plenty of things that needed fixing, of course. So, what did I change this time?

I made a few final decision calls: I do think the *zapatillas* in question are probably slippers rather than sneakers, and I think this particular *sirvienta* is most likely a maid rather than a housekeeper, and so on. I could keep on doubting these things for ever, but the translation's got to be finished one day, so at some point I've just got to commit. (H/T to Chilean stepdad for help with these two decisions in particular.)

Several changes in this pass were made based entirely on sound. I always tell early-career translators how essential it is to read their work out loud, yet do it myself embarrassingly rarely; but like many people, I do sort of read out loud *in my head*; which is to say, I have a sense of the sound of things even if my reading is ostensibly silent; so even without vocalising the text, I make changes that are for no obvious reason other than what the words sound like in my mind's ear. I changed *wrapped in a worn blanket* to *wrapped in a worn old blanket*, because the first one "sounded" too much like it was about a *warm* blanket. I notice repetitions because they jar aurally, too: *For a little while I massage your hand, but later, when I have* ~~handed it back~~ *returned it to you, I notice how you relax*. I changed a *whole* to an *entire* only because it was too near a *hole* on the page for the former to be inconspicuous. I changed a *starting* to a *beginning*, just because I wanted an extra syllable. When this translation is published, I will occasionally find myself called upon to read bits of it aloud – usually at festivals or other public events – and I want it to be ready for me.

In an early edit, I might need to stop and think and rephrase every sentence; at this late stage, I can whizz through much faster, and the speed does itself help me to notice things. I came to a little phrase on page 161 that rang a faint bell – *hmm, I've seen this before*, I thought – and on a quick check, yes, it had indeed appeared previously on page 24. Because there was only a day or so separating my reading of page 24 from my reading of page 161, the former was sufficiently fresh that I remembered it. I had never noticed that particular little echo before, when working much more slowly. (I still don't know how to make this one work in English, incidentally, but at least I now know it's there.)

As usual, there were several moments in this reading where I marked my manuscript with a **[chk]** because I still needed to check back against the original, usually because it was clear that there was *something* funny going on but I couldn't tell what... In two cases I found I had simply made a mistake; in the others, I needed to ensure that any strangeness of mine was a match for any strangeness of Diamela's – the solution in such cases isn't to make it *not* strange, the solution is to figure out how to keep it strange but make it work anyway. So many of Diamela's sentences surprise you – unusual things are connected to one another, sometimes there's even a switch in speaker mid-sentence and it's not always clear exactly where the pivot comes – so I wanted to be certain that any such curiosities in my text were only reflections of comparable ones in hers. My two weeks' absence has helped me to be a <u>reader</u> of this book, to respond like a reader, to be entranced by it (with any luck) or occasionally thrown by what it's doing – in which case I can learn from that response and act upon it.

The English book is currently 48,342 words long. If you're keeping score, that means it's down another 80 words since the last read. Meanwhile, the number of asterisks – marking my problems still outstanding – has fallen to 78. So what are they?

Well, in a small number of cases, they're simply things I <u>do not understand</u>. There are maybe three or four sentences in the book where, try as I might, I just cannot fathom what's going on. I might need to ask the author about these, ultimately. There are also a few asterisks marking places where I do know what's going on in the Spanish, but still need to figure out an adequate solution in the English: I still need a word that works in this particular instance for the troublesome Spanish adjective "moreno"; I still need to figure out a clever rephrasing of an existing line that doesn't reveal the gender of its subject too early; and so on.

Most of the remaining asterisks, though, mark the presence of Spanish words whose meanings I know perfectly well, but where I'm still wavering between (sometimes very different) English options for the specific context – a verb whose subject could be "I" or "he" and I have to decide which is more likely in the context; an adjective that might mean "precise" or "necessary" and either could fit within the context; a verb that could be "haunts" or "grieves" – either could work, but I need to choose for this particular context; a noun that is either "conscience" or "awareness", but in the specific context, my choice of one or the other would have divergent implications. (Have I mentioned that context is quite important?)

This last category of problems – words I know, but for which I need to decide between option A and option B – I have just sent to Carolina, at the publishers, to canvas her thoughts. Since she knows the book well, I'd be interested to see whether in each of these last few dozen cases, her instincts are the same as mine – essentially just a useful little sense check. In the coming days, I'll find out Caro's thoughts on those particular doubts, and I'll resolve whatever I have outstanding. If necessary, the author will get one more e-mail, if anything still remains intransigent after that. The last problems should be solved – and the final asterisks eliminated – by Friday.

Then I will read it all once through this weekend, and deliver the finished version to Charco Press next Monday. For this final read, I have changed the whole manuscript from Constantia (my usual working font) to Calibri (an unremarkable sans-serif one); I've closed the line spaces and widened all the margins so the text sits in the middle of the page, a bit more like a regular book. I always make some cosmetic changes for the final read – the font change is the most normal one – which helps me to notice quite different things (once the alignments are all changed), and generally to see it fresh.

All being well, I will write again next Monday to report that the book is DONE.

In the meantime, I'll share a finished-ish page with you.

9 May (2)

An Unpleasant Example for You

Between the penultimate read (this past weekend) and the final read (next weekend), I thought I'd share another bit of actual text, so you can perhaps get a better sense of what on earth I've been on about, on a slightly less micro scale than usual. You'll see how some of Diamela's sentences work, how they lead you on, double back, surprise you with observations and word choices. It may look like there's great exactness in what we're being told, yet at each moment in the sentence, the author contrives to keep her reader constantly uncertain. (I love this about the book.)

In the scene below, the narrator describes two people dying after they've been shot in a bank robbery. Be warned: it's a little gruesome, so don't read it if you're squeamish. But if you do, you'll see a good example of one of the effects the book pulls off repeatedly – what might look like an emotional coolness, an apparent distance, but charged with physical detail that's relentlessly unflinching. It's quite an effect when sustained.

(There's another scene in which a stranger has been horribly wounded in a traffic accident, but it's told from the perspective of the narrator who's stuck on a bus that's been held up by this accident and she's worrying about arriving at work on time. It's so good.)

Here you go, then – we're now not quite at the *final* final version, but very nearly. See what you think…

Beside my window the sirens howl. I understand that, further off, in the next neighbourhood, a shooting has occurred, a bank robbery. One of the bullets was a direct hit on the security guard, a man of about thirty, in his blue uniform, dark-skinned, but, no, not slim. A guard who prior to the gunshot had a presence. Yes, he'd had a presence because he was a diligent, silent, armed man. But now the guard falls to the floor, on his side, foetal, curled up, fatally wounded. Death, his own, lodged in the misery of one of his lungs and through the hole, due to the precision of the gunshot, through the irreversible severity of the wound, the blood rushes, a blood that is common and current, though hindered by the tireless clots that ruin the most watery elegance that has always characterised red. Amid a minor or almost derisory or anodyne agony the guard is dying and the woman dies too, killed by her stupid hunger for the limelight. She dies irreversibly, strewn slowly across the floor, she's dying from two, three well-aimed shots to the head. She dies and she dies as though she were the only creature in the entire universe.

She dies inwardly, confused.

She agonizes, convulsing.

And she jumps about, stretched out on the

ground, because the bullets in her head compel her to these absurd, uncontrolled movements, and there, the encephalic mass, a significant part of her brains, they slide over the floor of the bank, dirtying its tidy ground. It is dirtied and degraded by this thick, impure matter that drains out of the perishing head of the woman who is dying and dying in a savage act that does not horrify but rather provokes nausea. The public spectacle of this woman of, how old?, around forty, forty-five, what does it matter, a uniformed executive, nervous when faced with a robbery, who didn't know how to or couldn't withdraw or didn't want to keep out of the theft let alone do without screaming and didn't forgo insults either, and didn't, she just didn't, hide her haughty contempt for the robbers, until the two or three bullets brought her down, her eyes rolled upwards, the convulsions, legs mobile and final, the ludicrous-ness of a body governed by its own neurology, the surprising workings of the body. The woman dies more quickly or more noisily than the guard, they both die pervaded by different signs. The guard more modest, more committed or circumspect or absent in the minutes of his death, so different from the bullets of the convulsive woman, with abstract neurons scattered on a floor that could no longer be considered pristine.

Oh, how these oppressive sirens scare us.

The ambulances seem to be connected to the police's fast cars. All the bodies: the doctors and the repressive silhouettes of a frigid state police, step in the organic matter, ruin the death rattles of the brain-less woman and don't pause at this abject contaminated ground, no, they don't, and nor do they feel sorry for the guard who still hasn't finished dying, who is clinging to himself, although he's already dead, he is, so the doctor will declare him with all his vast meticulous indifference. Both of them pallid, astonishingly pale, animated only by the noticeable trickles of blood adorning them. And oh, the bank invaded by the police forces and the medical teams and the encephalic mass of the woman and the active urgency of the teams that move, spurred on or vigorous, faced with a blood that excites them, and validates them.

It often feels as though a translation will never be finished, like it'll never even get close. The very idea that one might adequately translate something – I mean, even the notion of re-making a whole complex text, in detail, out of totally different words – seems impossible. But we do it anyway.

Nearly there now.

10 May

Supporting Materials

Just a little supplement to yesterday's post.

For the purposes of comparison, if you read Spanish, here's the opening paragraph:

> Al lado de mi ventana resuena el ulular de las sirenas. Comprendo que, más allá, en el barrio adyacente, se ha consumado una balacera, el asalto al banco. Una de las balas dio directo en el guardia, un hombre de unos treinta años, vestido con su uniforme azul, moreno, aunque no esbelto, no. Un guardia que antes del balazo tuvo una presencia. Sí, la tuvo porque era un hombre armado, silencioso y diligente. Observador, silencioso y diligente. Armado. Pero ahora el guardia cae al suelo, de costado, fetal, acurrucado, herido de muerte. La muerte, la suya, alojada en la miseria de uno de sus pulmones y por el hueco, debido a la exactitud del balazo, por la gravedad irreversible de la herida, se precipita la sangre, una sangre común y corriente, aunque

entorpecida por los infatigables coágulos que arruinan la prestancia más acuosa que siempre ha caracterizado al rojo. En medio de una agonía leve o casi irrisoria o anodina está muriendo el guardia y muere también la mujer, la mata su estúpido afán de protagonismo. Muere irreversible, lentamente tirada en el suelo, está muriendo de dos, tres certeros balazos en su cabeza. Muere y muere como si fuera la única criatura en todo el universo.

And for the purposes of reassurance, here's where this bit started in English, a couple of months back:

Beside my window RESUENA the ULULAR [howl] of the sirens. I understand that, MAS ALLA, in the next neighbourhood, a BALACERA has CONSU-MADO, a bank robbery. One of the bullets DIO DIRECTO EN the security guard, a man of about thirty, in his blue uniform, MORENO [dark/tan] but, no, not ESBELTO [slim?]. A guard who before the BALAZO had a presence. Yes, he had a presence because he was a DILIGENTE, silent, armed man. But now the guard falls to the floor, DE COSTADO, foetal, ACURRUCADO, HERIDO DE MUERTE [fatally wounded?]. Death, his, ALOJADA [lodged?] in the MISERIA of one of his lungs and POR EL HUECO, due to the precision of the BALAZO, POR the irreversible severity of the wound, the blood SE PRECIPITA, a blood that is common and CORRIENTE, though ENTORPECIDA by the INFATIGABLES COAGULOS that ARRUINAN the most watery PRESTANCIA that has always characterised EL ROJO [red - no art.?]. Amid a LEVE or almost IRRISORIA or ANODINA agony the guard is dying and LA MUJER dies too, she is killed by his* stupid AFAN DE PROTAGONISMO. She dies IRREVERSIBLE, slowly TIRADA on the floor, she's dying from two, three well-aimed BALAZOS to the head. She dies and she dies as though she were the only creature in the whole universe.

Ah, feels like only yesterday.

16 May

Delivery Day

I am writing this entry at 5:25 p.m., on Sunday the 16th of May.

When I began this diary, three and a half months ago, I had not yet read Diamela Eltit's *Jamás el fuego nunca*. In my first entry, I told you I was beginning a process that would probably involve coming to know that novel, temporarily, better than any other book in the world – and most likely falling gradually in love with it, as that close familiarity increased.

If you've been following this diary, you'll know that the whole translation process has been slightly slower than expected. The book was longer than I'd realised, and a lot more difficult, and I was distracted by too many other things along the way. But as of a couple of minutes ago, I've got a translation of it that's finished. Or at least "finished". I started with what was (as I discovered) a really great original book; then it became deeply, chaotically awful from the moment I first laid hands on it, and it remained so for quite a while (throughout much of the translation process); and draft by draft has been slowly edging back towards being good again. And now it's back in focus, with images and prose that, while complex, have a sharpness to them, and it's where I want it to be. It's not the same book it was, translation is never quite that, not ever, but I think it's as good as I can make it.

As I mentioned when describing my penultimate read-through last week, I have been progressively acquiring a sense of what Diamela sounds like in English, coherently, in this piece of work. Even one single book, when inhabited so intensively for a few months, can reveal a lot about a writer. (I've ordered copies of the four previous English translations of her other books and am curious to investigate how those voices compare with my version.) If I ever have the good fortune to translate another of Diamela's novels, I'm sure there are many things this book will have taught me that I'll carry over.

(Last week I translated an extract of a new novel by a writer I've been working with forever, collaborating on seven or eight books. There was a word in the text I was sure I'd never seen before, and which I couldn't find explained in any dictionary or online reference, so I wrote to him to ask. His very sweet reply began, in the manner of an elderly spouse, *I'm glad I can still surprise you with a word now and then even after all these years…*)

When I wrote in late January that I would come to know this book very well, I assumed I'd also come to *understand* it. But it hasn't quite worked out that way, because I don't think it's that sort of book. I believe I have a good sense of what the author is *doing*, but there are parts of the book itself I'm not sure I do understand, if I'm honest. In other circumstances, that might worry me. (Or at least, worry me enough not to admit the failing quite as publicly as this.) But one of the things I *have* come to understand is that this particular author seems quite comfortable with doubt. More than that, the writing actively encourages it. I've mentioned textual ambiguity many times in this diary – the first reference appeared back on January 28, and I discussed it in the most detail on March 14 and April 22; and I think I was somehow groping clumsily towards one of the novel's defining characteristics – and, perhaps, the novelist's. I am not reassured by what she writes, and it offers or confirms no certainties, but I am utterly, constantly *intrigued* by it; and if she is comfortable with doubt, then, well, as a reader, I need to learn how to be, too. It's not something we encourage very often in novels (or outside novels). I think it is brilliant.

So what have I done since I last wrote in this diary, what has this concluding stage involved?

Well, this weekend I've had a look at the helpful thoughts Caro sent me on the last of my outstanding queries (she and I had roughly the same reading of the problematic bits about three-quarters of the time, which helps to put my mind at ease). And having worked the list of still intransigent words down to just thirteen, I've sent my patient author an e-mail to learn her thinking on these; they're mostly very common words that I absolutely know, but I'm struggling to tell what she's doing with them in their particular context. I'll be curious to see what she says. Though since everything else in the translation is now done, I'm not going to wait for her last little responses before I deliver it – it'll only require changing a handful of words at most, so I can drop those changes in at a later stage if any of my eleventh-hour hunches prove to have been wildly wrong.

I've also, as planned, read the whole book from end to end one final time, pretty briskly, tinkering with it in tiny ways – maybe one or two micro changes per page. This included a few more cases of reversing where I'd previously by instinct used phrasal verbs, as discussed a little in the second entry on April 5. (In the sentence "Now I set the biscuit down on the plate, I get up and take the handbag off the nail, I sit back down at the table, I put on my glasses and look for my notebook", *set down*, *get up*, *take off*, *sit down*, *put on* and *look for* are each a single word in Spanish.) In one instance I've finally decided to allow a brand-new ambiguity into the translation – a *still* that could mean *yet* or *motionless*, both of them appropriate – which isn't in the original but I'm embracing the fact that English allows it, and it's totally *in the spirit of* the original. Oh, and I also bit the bullet and deleted an entire sentence on page 100. (The original harbours a clever ambiguity here, and I needed to excise a whole line of dialogue in order to construct something that retained it. It's barely a momentary doubt in my version, compared to several lines of sustained effect in the Spanish, but I hope it's enough at least to unbalance a reader just briefly.)

So I am now about to send my translation to Carolina and Sam at the publishers, along with my invoice (this part is <u>very important</u>), and oh, now I will – oh help – cross my fingers that they don't hate it. And if –

But – no. That's not altogether honest. The truth is, I do actually think they'll like it, because I do believe it's a very good piece of work. I'm absolutely not immune to self-doubt, nor to impostor syndrome, and they've both certainly had a decent work-out in these past few months, more for this book than most; but there are also parts of the process where, you know, I do think I'm *not* bad at this. I said in my first entry that I was going to tell the truth in this diary, and well, the absolute truth this evening is that I *don't* secretly think it's rubbish and everyone's going to hate it and I'm going to be found out at last. No, the truth is that this evening I'm rather proud of this bit of work.

I know: smug, but true.

So. Tonight the manuscript has gone back into Constantia, 12-point, 1.5-spaced, I've done a search for any surviving note-to-self asterisks or square brackets (none!), checked there are no rogue double-spaces anywhere to be found, and the file name has been changed from *Diamela EN live draft* to *Diamela EN final*. At close of play, the tally is 48,198 words. (Other essential building blocks include a total of 5,362 commas. The original had 5,242, which is close enough.)

Looking back over this book, it does seem as though an unusual number of those words (and commas) gave me trouble. And even after these many drafts and redrafts, the translation is not really finished, of course. But it's got as far as it's going to get without intervention from anyone else, which is why this is the right time for me to relinquish my sole control of it; now comes the edit, the first of several collaborative engagements which I'm sure will make it better in lots of ways.

For now, though, the main bit of *my* work is done.

I'm very grateful to everyone who's accompanied me along the way, especially to those of you who sent me messages or tweets, or who commented on the blog, those of you who asked questions or offered suggestions.[39] Weird as this sharing has been, I've enjoyed the company. Thanks, too, to my friends at Charco for not thinking this was a terrible idea (or perhaps thinking it but kindly not telling me as much); and to my author, for allowing me to draw back the curtain on the process, and most of all for entrusting her truly remarkable book to me, to be dismantled and reconstructed in entirely different words.

---

[39] Most specifically, thanks to Vineet Lal, Daniel Steele, Anne McLean, Anne Rooney, Hilary McKay, Sabine Citron, Marina Sofia and Lara Bourdin for allowing their comments/messages to be quoted in this book.

This brand-new incarnation is called *Never Did the Fire*, it's written by Diamela Eltit and now translated by me. I can't wait for you to read it.

Right – it's attached. I'm clicking SEND.

Afterword

And there the online post-by-post publication of this diary ends, on 16 May 2021, at the point where the novel seemed – at last, after all those terrible drafts – to be blazing back into life, and so the manuscript felt ready to be delivered to the publisher. Though, of course, that's never the end of the process. There would be a couple of rounds of edits, there would be proofs to read, a cover design, promotional plans around the launch, and then, at last, publication day. And even publication day, about ten months after the delivery date, is itself more of a beginning than an ending – because what comes afterwards are the book-sellers and librarians and reviewers, and of course, the readers. Most of those who come to read my translation will be people who could not access Diamela's novel in Spanish; the aim of my translation, and the reason for all the fuss it's taken me to get there, is to allow them a proxy experience that's as precisely the same as that other book as possible, in all its brilliant, ambiguous complexity. If you're one of those readers, I hope you find it so.

I began the Introduction to this book with the straight-for-ward question: what actually does being a literary translator entail? It's a question to which every translator I know would offer a somewhat different answer. This diary, to the best of my ability, was mine.

When I set out on this diary, I intended it, principally, for a readership of interested non-translators, as an attempt to demystify something that *I* think is fascinating and I hoped others would, too. I imagined there wouldn't be much in it that long-serving professionals would find new, but I hoped that those without any translation experience of their own might find it revealing. As it turned out, though, while I was indeed delighted to hear from many non-translator readers ("Wait, whoah, you people have to do *what*?" – yeah, we do this thing so you don't have to...), a fair number of translators read it, too, and their reactions were instructive. For the most part, what they expressed was not surprise but solidarity and especially a sense of – what – reassurance? So many friends wrote to say "I'm so glad I'm not the only one who finds that part of it really difficult"; or even "Wow, can't tell you how thrilled I am – your first drafts are even worse than mine!" (This exposure, a necessary part of honest, warts-and-all sharing, might explain Anne's reference to "bravery" way back in January.) I don't think we talk about our processes enough, about the difficulties we find in them; so if my various troubles and incompetencies helped others to come to terms with their own, that will have been a thing worth doing.

The truth is, like any writing that aspires to complexity, translation can feel like a pointless, wretched struggle. The voice doesn't come, things get more and more hesitant and tangled, your language simply won't do what you want it to, and before you know it the cow has gone to the swamp. (As they say in Brazil. I'd translate that as "it's all gone pear-shaped".) And yet sometimes, when it's going well, it feels like it's really *my* piece of writing. (But is it? On that, I'm in two minds.[40])

The first comment I received after posting my final entry kindly expressed some confidence in how good the translation would surely be, based on all the reflection that went into it

---

[40] As a translator, this is where I spend a lot of my time.

in the diary. And while I'm grateful for this confidence, I do wonder how much the reflection that goes into writing about the practice does indeed help to improve the practice – it's an interesting question. There are certainly things I've done a bit differently because I've had to think about them in a way that would allow me to articulate and explain them; but I also believe (and fervently hope) that a good translation doesn't *require* this sort of real-time self-scrutiny. I'll keep pondering that one.

What I am sure of, though, is that close examining of translation does at least make translation more *interesting*, not less. I was never really taught to translate, so any deliberate thinking I've done about it has been frankly pretty slapdash. Much of it has happened in the process of teaching translation to others, and examining other people's prose. But in this diary I had to examine not only my texts, and some of the individual choices I referred to in the Introduction, but also my own mind at work – my deductive processes, my reading experience, my instincts. A process like this can help to structure one's own doubts, too – and expressing the quite rigorous demands made on oneself, well, in a funny way it's almost heartening.

Translating a poorly written text that's lacking in clarity is always hard and frustrating, and so it is with the process of articulating one's own thoughts: clear articulating demands clarity of thinking, so combining my self-examination with a need to record and *express* my discoveries compelled me to much greater focus. (If some of what you've read in this book still seemed blurry and undisciplined, all I can say is that that, too, is at least an honest representation of what was going on in my head. Believe me when I tell you, it could have been a whole lot worse.) If you, who are reading this, happen to be a translator, I would strongly recommend it, this curious self-scrutiny. But learn from my bad example and maybe don't try it on such a bloody difficult book, though?

Lewes, December 2021

INDEX

adjectives, multiple, 38-9, 81-2, 95-6

admissions of defeat, 129, 165-6

ambiguity, author's use of, 101-2, 164-5, 197

ambiguity, avoiding unintentional, 97, 154, 164-5

ambiguity, preserving intentional, 28, 46, 59-60, 86, 100-2, 160, 164-6, 198

articles, definite and indefinite, 57-9, 156

asterisks, translator's use of, 142

author, involvement of, 163, 181, 185

authorial DNA, 10, 79-80, 132

Beatles, The, 15-16

car crashes (actual, in the novel), 129, 159-60

car crashes (figurative, utter, in the translation), 26, 67-8, etc.

cheese sandwich, making a, 6

Child, Lauren, 71, 73

Chilenismos, 27, 37-8, 121, 124, 128, 151, 159, 167

Cien años de soledad, 27, 61, 173f; see also *One Hundred Years of Solitude*

Communist Manifesto, The, 114, 121

context, 28, 38, 39, 58, 90, 111, 118-9, 124, 128, 134, 149, 156, 174, 184

contractions, 135, 139, 145, 158

CHARCO PRESS

Director & Editor: Carolina Orloff
Director: Samuel McDowell

www.charcopress.com

Catching Fire was published on
80gsm Munken Premium Cream paper.

The text was designed using Bembo 11.5 and ITC Galliard.

Printed in January 2022 by TJ Books
Padstow, Cornwall, PL28 8RW using responsibly
sourced paper and environmentally-friendly adhesive.